INTER
BILLI

Life is a game o̶... ̶ ̶p̶l̶e̶a̶s̶u̶r̶e̶.
And these men play to win!

Let Modern™ Romance take you on a jet-set journey
to meet eight male wonders of the world.
From rich tycoons to royal playboys—
they're red-hot and ruthless!

International Billionaires coming in 2009

The Prince's Waitress Wife
by Sarah Morgan, February.

At the Argentinean Billionaire's Bidding
by India Grey, March.

The French Tycoon's Pregnant Mistress
by Abby Green, April.

The Ruthless Billionaire's Virgin
by Susan Stephens, May.

The Italian Count's Defiant Bride
by Catherine George, June.

The Sheikh's Love-Child
by Kate Hewitt, July.

Blackmailed into the Greek Tycoon's Bed
by Carol Marinelli, August.

The Virgin Secretary's Impossible Boss
by Carol Mortimer, September.

8 volumes in all to collect!

Dear Reader

The opportunity to combine two passions doesn't come along very often, but when the editors hinted at a series of books to celebrate the 6 Nations Rugby tour, I was instantly buzzing with excitement. I hold season tickets for one of the top teams in this country, which reflects my passion for the game.

Having been a professional singer, the chance to write about a young girl about to perform the national anthem in front of the crowd before the start of the match, was a gift. Having that young girl rescued after suffering a wardrobe malfunction by the team's most reclusive supporter was the moment I knew I had to write the book.

Being part of this series along with some of your favourite authors was the icing on the cake for me, and I just know you're going to love each new book.

A young singer *and* rugby? A perfect combination for me.

A young woman with supreme talent and very little experience of life outside of her musical cocoon and a man whose sporting career has been tragically foreshortened, leaving him scarred inside and out…

That sounds like the seeds of a love story to me.

I do hope you enjoy Ethan and Savannah's story, and please remember I love nothing more than hearing from my readers around the world!

www.susanstephens.net

Happy reading everyone!

Susan

THE RUTHLESS BILLIONAIRE'S VIRGIN

BY
SUSAN STEPHENS

MILLS & BOON®

Pure reading pleasure™

First published in Great Britain 2009
Harlequin Mills & Boon Limited,
Eton House, 18-24 Paradise Road, Richmond, Surrey TW9 1SR

© Harlequin Books SA 2009

Special thanks and acknowledgement are given to Susan Stephens

ISBN: 978 0 263 87201 9

Set in Times Roman 10¾ on 12¼ pt
01-0509-47183

Printed and bound in Spain
by Litografia Rosés, S.A., Barcelona

Susan Stephens was a professional singer before meeting her husband on the tiny Mediterranean island of Malta. In true Modern™ Romance style they met on Monday, became engaged on Friday and were married three months after that. Almost thirty years and three children later, they are still in love. (Susan does not advise her children to return home one day with a similar story, as she may not take the news with the same fortitude as her own mother!)

Susan had written several non-fiction books when fate took a hand. At a charity costume ball there was an after-dinner auction. One of the lots, 'Spend a Day with an Author', had been donated by Mills & Boon® author Penny Jordan. Susan's husband bought this lot, and Penny was to become not just a great friend but a wonderful mentor, who encouraged Susan to write romance.

Susan loves her family, her pets, her friends and her writing. She enjoys entertaining, travel and going to the theatre. She reads, cooks, and plays the piano to relax, and can occasionally be found throwing herself off mountains on a pair of skis or galloping through the countryside. Visit Susan's website: www.susanstephens.net—she loves to hear from her readers all around the world!

CHAPTER ONE

SOME said confidence was the most potent aphrodisiac of all, but for the man the world of rugby called 'the Bear', confidence was only a starting point. Confidence took courage, something Ethan Alexander proved he had each time he faced the world with his disfiguring scars.

A change swept over the Stadio Flaminio in Rome when Ethan took his seat to watch Italy play England in the Six Nations rugby tournament. Men sat a little straighter, while women flicked their hair as they moistened their immaculately made-up lips.

Without the Bear, any match, even an international fixture like this one, lacked the frisson of danger Ethan carried with him. Tall, dark, and formidably scarred, Ethan was more than an avid rugby supporter, he was an unstoppable tycoon, a man who defied the standards by which other men were judged. His face might be damaged, but Ethan possessed a blistering glamour born of keen intelligence and a steely will. His grey eyes blazed with an internal fire women longed to feel scorch them, and men wished they could harness, but today that passion had ebbed into simmering frustration as he contemplated human frailty. How could something as simple as a sore throat lead a world-famous diva like Madame de Silva to pull out of singing the national anthem for England at such an event as this?

The same way a damaged spine could end his own career as a professional rugby player, Ethan's inner voice informed him with brutal honesty.

He'd brought in a young singer as a replacement for Madame de Silva. Savannah Ross had recently been signed to the record company he ran as a hobby to reflect his deep love of music. He hadn't met Savannah, but Madame de Silva had recommended her, and his marketing people were touting the young singer as the next big thing.

Next big thing maybe, but Savannah Ross was late on pitch. He flashed a glance at the stadium clock that counted down the seconds. Hiring an inexperienced girl for an important occasion like this only reminded him why he never took risks. He'd thought it a good idea to give his new signing a break; now he wasn't so sure. Could Savannah Ross come up with the goods? She better had. She'd been flown here on his private jet and he'd been told she'd arrived. So where was she?

Ethan frowned as he shifted his powerful frame. The execution of last-minute formalities was timed to the second to accommodate a global television audience. No allowances could be made for inexperience, and *he* wouldn't allow for last-minute nerves. Savannah Ross had accepted this engagement, and now she must perform.

This wasn't like any theatre she'd ever played in before, or any concert-hall either. It was a bleak, tiled tunnel filled with the scent of sweaty feet and tension. She didn't even have a proper dressing-room to get changed in—not that she minded, because it was such an honour to be here. Hard to believe she would soon be singing the national anthem on the pitch for the England rugby squad—or at least she would once she found someone to tell her where she was supposed to go and when.

Poking her head through the curtain of the 'dressing-room' she'd been allocated, Savannah called out. No one answered. Not surprising, in this shadowy tunnel leading to the pitch. The lady who had issued Savannah with a visitor's pass at the entrance had explained to her that what rooms there were would be needed for the teams and their support staff. Knowing Madame de Silva always travelled in style with an entourage, including Madame's hairdresser and the girl whose job it was to care for Madame's pet chihuahua, Savannah guessed the management of the stadium had been only too relieved to release the many rooms Madame would have taken up. And she was grateful for what she had: an adjunct to the tunnel—a hole in the wall, really—an alcove over which somebody had hastily draped a curtain.

And she had more important things on her mind than her comfort, like the clock ticking away the seconds before the match. She had definitely been forgotten, which was understandable. Taking Madame's place had been so last-minute, and her signing to the record label so recent, that no one knew her. How could anyone be expected to recognise or remember her? And though she had been guided to this alcove everyone had rushed off, leaving her with no idea what she was supposed to do. Sing? Yes, that was obvious, but when should she walk onto the pitch? And was she supposed to wait for someone to come back to escort her, or should she just march out there?

Hearing the chanting of the excited crowd, Savannah knew she must find help. She was about to do just that when she heard the rumble of conversation coming closer. A group of businessmen was striding down the tunnel and they must pass her curtained alcove. She would ask one of them what to do.

'Excuse me—' Savannah's enquiry was cut short as— whoosh, splat!—she was flattened against the wall like an invisible fly. The men were so busy talking they hadn't even noticed her as they'd thundered past, talking about the man they called the Bear, a man who had made his own way to his seat when all of them had been jostling to be the one to escort him.

The Bear…

Savannah shivered involuntarily. That was the nickname of the tycoon who had sent his jet to fetch her. Ethan Alexander, rugby fanatic and international billionaire, was an unattached and unforgettable man, a shadowy figure who regularly featured in the type of magazines Savannah bought when she wanted to drool over unattainable men. No one yet had gained a clear insight into Ethan's life, though speculation was rife, and of course, the more he shunned publicity, the more intriguing the public found him.

She really must stop thinking about Ethan Alexander and concentrate on her predicament. To save time she would put on her gown and then go hunting for help.

But even the sight of her beautiful gown failed to divert Savannah's thoughts from Ethan. From what the men had said about him, having Ethan at the match was akin to having royalty turn up—or maybe even better, because he was an undisputed king amongst men. Taking into account the man-mountains in the England team, the Bear was the best of all the men there, they said; he was the deadliest in the pack.

Savannah shivered at the thought of so much undiluted maleness. By the time she had wriggled her way into her gown she had worked herself into a state of debilitating nerves, though she reasoned it wasn't surprising she was intimidated, when this tunnel led onto the pitch where the atmosphere was humming with testosterone and almost palpable aggression.

The thought took her straight back to Ethan. The power he threw off, even from the printed page, made him physically irresistible. Perhaps it was the steely will in his eyes, or the fact he was such a powerfully built man. He might be a lot older than she was, and terribly scarred, but she wasn't the only woman who thought Ethan's injuries only made him more compelling. In magazine polls he was regularly voted the man most women wanted to go to bed with.

Not that someone as inexperienced as her should be dwelling on that. No, Savannah told herself firmly, she was gripped more by the aura of danger and tragedy surrounding Ethan. In her eyes his scars only made him seem more human and real.

Oh, really? Savannah's cynical-self interrupted. *So that would be why these 'innocent' thoughts of yours regularly trigger enough sensation to start a riot?*

Prudently, Savannah refused to answer that. She had no time for any of these distractions. She poked her head round the curtain again. There was still no one there, and she was fast running out of options. If she continued to yell she'd have no voice left for singing. If she put her jeans on again and went looking for help, she'd be late onto the pitch. But she couldn't let Madame de Silva down, who had recommended her for this important occasion. She couldn't let down the squad, or Ethan Alexander, the man who had employed her. She'd put her dress on, then at least she'd be ready. Or her parents who had scrimped and saved to buy the dress for her, and she only wished they could be here with her now. Secretly she was happiest on the farm with them, up to her knees in mud in a pair of Wellington boots, but she would never trample on their dreams for her by telling them that.

As her mother's anxious face swam into her mind, Savannah realised it wasn't singing in front of a world-wide audience that terrified her, but the possibility that something might go wrong to embarrass her parents. She loved them dearly. Like many farmers they'd had it so hard when the deadly foot-and-mouth disease had wiped out their cattle. Her main ambition in life now was to make them smile again.

Savannah tensed, hearing her name mentioned on the tannoy system. And when the announcer described her in over-sugary terms, as the girl with the golden tonsils and hair to match, she grimaced, thinking it the best case she'd ever heard for dyeing her hair bright pink. The crowd disagreed and applauded wildly, which only convinced Savannah that when they saw her in person she could only disappoint. Far from being the dainty blonde the build-up had suggested, she was a fresh-faced country girl with serious self-confidence issues—and one who right now would rather be anywhere else on earth than here.

Pull yourself together! Savannah told herself impatiently. This gown had cost a fortune her parents could scarcely afford. Was she going to let them down? She started to struggle with the zip. The gown had been precision-made to fit her fuller figure, and was in her favourite colour, pink. With the aid of careful draping it didn't even make her look fat. It was all in the cut and the boning, her mother had explained, which was why they always travelled up to the far north of England for Savannah's fittings, where there were dressmakers who knew about such things.

'You can't wear that!'

Savannah jumped back as her curtain was ripped aside. 'Do you mind?' she exclaimed, modestly covering her chest at the sight of a man whose physique perfectly matched his reedy voice. 'Why can't I wear it?' she protested, tightening her arms over her chest. It was a beautiful dress, but the man was looking at it as if it were a bin liner with holes cut in it for her head and arms.

'You just can't,' he said flatly.

Taking in the official England track-suit he was wearing, Savannah curbed her tongue, but she wasn't prepared to let the man continue with the peep show he seemed intent on having, and she held the curtain tightly around her. 'What's wrong with it?' she asked with all the politeness she could muster.

'It's not appropriate—and if I tell you that you can't wear it then you can't.'

What a bully, she thought, and her flesh crawled as the man continued to stare at her curvy form behind the flimsy curtain. Did he mean the neckline was too low? She always had trouble hiding her breasts, and as she'd got older she hated the way men stared at them. She would be the first to acknowledge her chest was currently displayed to best advantage in the low-cut gown, but it was a performance outfit. She could hardly hide her large breasts under her arms! 'Not appropriate *how*?' she said, standing her ground.

The man's disappointment that she didn't fold immediately was all too obvious. 'The Bear won't approve of it,' he said, as if that was the death knell of any hopes she had of wearing it.

'The Bear won't approve?' Savannah's heart fluttered a warning. To walk out onto the pitch and have Ethan Alexander stare at her… She had dreamed of it, but now it was going to happen she was losing confidence fast. That didn't mean she wouldn't defend her dress to kingdom come. 'I don't understand. Why wouldn't he approve of it?'

'It's pink,' the man said, his face twisting as if pink came with a bad smell.

Savannah's face crumpled. It was such a beautiful dress, and one her mother had been so thrilled to buy for her. They had discussed the fact that hours of dedicated work had gone into the hand-stitching alone, and now this man was dismissing the handiwork of craftswomen in a few unkind words.

'You'll have to take it off.'

'What?' Savannah felt the cold wall pressing against her back.

'I understand you're a last-minute replacement,' the man said in a kinder tone, which Savannah found almost creepier than his original hectoring manner. 'So you won't know that a major sponsor has supplied a designer gown for the occasion, which he expects to be worn. The dress has received more publicity than you have,' the man added unkindly.

'I'm not surprised,' Savannah muttered to herself. Well, it could hardly have received less, she thought wryly, seeing as she was a last-minute replacement. She kept a pleasant expression on her face, determined she wouldn't give this man the satisfaction of thinking he'd upset her.

'And the Bear expects all the sponsors, however small their donations, to get their fair share of publicity, so you'll have to wear it,' he finished crossly when she refused to capitulate.

Perhaps he would like her to cry so he could play the big man to her crushed little woman, Savannah reflected. If so, he was in for a disappointment. Because she was plump and rather short, people often mistook her for a sweet, plump, fluffy thing they could push around, when actually she could stick her arm up a cow and pull out a newborn calf during a difficult birth, something that had given her supreme joy on the few occasions she'd been called upon to do so. Her slender arms were kinder on a struggling mother, her father always said. She didn't come from the sort of background to be intimidated by a man who looked like he had a pole stuck up his backside.

'Well, if that's the dress I'm supposed to wear,' she said pragmatically, 'I'd better see it.' She hadn't come to Rome to cause ripples, but to do a job like anyone else, and the clock was ticking. Plus she was far too polite to say what she really wanted to say, which was *what the hell has it got to do with the Bear what I wear?*

Someone pretty important to your career, Savannah's sensible inner voice informed her as the man hurried off to get the dress; *someone who is both the main sponsor for the England squad and your boss.*

When he returned the man's manner had changed. Perhaps he believed he had worn her down, Savannah concluded.

'Madame Whatshername was pleased enough to wear it,' he said with a sniff as he handed the official gown over to Savannah.

Savannah paled as she held up Madame de Silva's

gown. She should have known it would be fitted to the great singer. Madame was half her size, and wore the type of couture dress favoured by French salon-society. The closest Savannah had ever come to a salon was the local hairdresser's, and her gowns were all geared towards comfort and big knickers. 'I don't think Madame's gown will fit me,' she muttered, losing all her confidence in a rush as she stared at the slim column of a dress with its fishtail train.

'Whether it fits you or not,' the man insisted, 'You have to wear it. I can't allow you onto the pitch wearing your dress when the sponsor is expecting to see his official gown worn. Putting his design in front of a worldwide television audience is the whole point of the exercise.'

With her in it? Savannah very much doubted that was what the designer had had in mind.

'You have to look the part,' the man insisted.

Of team jester? Savannah was starting to feel sick, and not just with pre-concert nerves. In farming lingo she would be classified as 'healthy breeding stock', whereas Madame de Silva was a slender greyhound, all sleek and toned. There was no chance the gown would fit her, or suit her freckled skin. 'I'll do my best,' she promised as her throat constricted.

'Good girl,' the man said approvingly.

Savannah's chin wobbled as she surveyed the garish gown. She was going to look like a fool, and beyond her little drama in the tunnel she could hear that the mood of the crowd had escalated to fever pitch in anticipation of the kick-off.

Where was she? Ethan frowned as he flashed another glance at his wristwatch. A hush of expectancy had swept the capacity crowd. It was almost time for the match to start, and he was more on edge than he had ever been. He had promised the squad a replacement singer, and now it looked as if Savannah Ross was going to let him down. In minutes the England team would be lining up in the tunnel, and the brass band was already out on the pitch. The portly tenor who had been booked to sing the anthem for Italy was busily accepting the plaudits of an adoring crowd, but where the hell was Savannah Ross?

Anxious glances shot Ethan's way. If the Bear was unhappy, everyone was unhappy, and Ethan was unusually tense.

Madame's fabulous form-fitting gown had a sash in bleakest white and ink-blot blue, which like a royal order was supposed to be worn over one naked shoulder.

Fabulous for Madame's slender frame, maybe, Savannah thought anxiously as she struggled to put the sash to better use. If she could just bite out these stitches, maybe, just maybe, she could spread out the fabric to cover the impending boob explosion—though up until now she had to admit her frantic plucking and gnawing had achieved nothing; try as she might, the sash refused to conceal any part of her bosom.

And as for the zip at the back...

Contorting her arms into a position that would have given Houdini a run for his money, she still couldn't do it up. Poking her head out of the curtain, she tried calling out again, but even the creepy man had deserted her. She peered anxiously down the tunnel. The crowd had grown quiet, which was a very bad sign. It meant the announcements were over and the match was about to start—and before that could happen she had to sing the national anthem! 'Hello! Is anyone—?'

'Hello,' a girl interrupted brightly, seemingly coming out of nowhere. 'Can I help you?'

After jumping about three feet in the air with shock, Savannah felt like kissing the ground the girl was about to walk on. 'If you could just get me into this dress...' Savannah knew it was a lost cause, but she had to try.

'Don't panic,' the girl soothed.

Savannah's saviour turned out to be a physiotherapist and was using the tones Savannah guessed she must have used a thousand times before, and in far more serious situations to reassure the injured players. 'I'm trying not to panic,' she admitted. 'But I'm so late, and the fact remains you can't fit a quart into a pint pot.'

The girl laughed with her. 'Let's see, shall we?'

The physio certainly knew all there was to know about manipulation, Savannah acknowledged gratefully when she was finally secured inside the dress. 'Don't worry, I'll be fine now,' she said, wiping her nose. 'That's if I don't burst out of it—!'

'You'll have a fair sized audience if you do,' the girl reminded her with a smile.

Yes, the crowd was wound up like a drum, and Savannah knew she would be in for a rough ride if anything went wrong out on the pitch.

As the physio collected up her things and wished her good luck, Savannah stared down in dismay at the acres of blood-red taffeta. It was just a shame every single one of those acres was in the wrong place. Madame was a lot taller than she was, and how she longed for the fabric collecting around her feet to be redistributed over her fuller figure. But it was too late to worry about that now.

'You'd better get out there,' the girl said, echoing these thoughts, 'Before you miss your cue.'

Don't tempt me! Savannah thought, testing whether it was possible to breathe, let alone sing, now she was pinned in. Barely, she concluded. She was trapped in a vice of couture stitching from which there was only one escape, and she didn't fancy risking that in front of the worldwide television audience. She'd much rather be safely back at home dreaming about Ethan Alexander rather than here on the pitch where he would almost certainly look at her and laugh.

But…

She braced herself.

The fact that she could hardly move, let alone breathe, didn't mean she couldn't use her legs, Savannah told herself fiercely as she tottered determinedly down the tunnel in a gown secured with safety pins, made for someone half her size.

Here goes nothing!

CHAPTER TWO

SHE had forgotten how much her diaphragm expanded when she let herself go and really raised the rafters. How could she have forgotten something as rudimentary as that?

Maybe because the massive crowd was a blur and all she was aware of was the dark, menacing shape of the biggest man on the benches behind the England sin bin, the area England players sat in when they were sent off the pitch for misdemeanours.

Sin.

She had to shake that thought off too, Savannah realised as she lifted her ribcage in preparation for commencing the rousing chorus. But how was she supposed to do that when she could feel Ethan's gaze in every fibre of her being? The moment she had walked onto the pitch she had known exactly where he was sitting, and who he was looking at. By the time she'd got over that, and the ear-splitting cheer that had greeted her, even the fear of singing in front of such a vast audience had paled into insignificance. And now she was trapped in a laser gaze that wouldn't let her go.

She really must shake off this presentiment of disaster, Savannah warned herself. Nervously moistening her lips, she took a deep breath. A very deep breath…

The first of several safety pins pinged free, and as the dress fell away it became obvious that the physio's pins were designed to hold bandages in place rather than acres of pneumatic flesh.

His mood had undergone a radical change from impatient to entranced, and all in a matter of seconds. The ruthless billionaire, as people liked to think of him, became a fan of his new young singing-sensation after hearing just a few bars of her music. The crowd agreed with him, judging by the way Savannah Ross had it gripped. When she had first stumbled onto the pitch, she had been greeted by wolf whistles and rowdy applause. At first he had thought her ridiculous too, with her breasts pouting over the top of the ill-fitting gown, but then he remembered the famous dress had been made for someone else, and that he should have found some way to warn her. But it was too late to worry about that now, and her appearance hardly mattered, for Savannah Ross had him and everyone else in the palm of her hand. She was so richly blessed with music it was all he could do to remain in his seat.

She refused to let the supporters down. She carried on regardless as more pins followed the first. She was expected to reflect the hopes and dreams of a country, and that was precisely what she was going to do—never mind the wretched dress letting her down. But as she prepared to sing the last few notes the worst happened—the final pin gave way and one pert breast sprang free, the generous swell of it nicely topped off with a rose-pink nipple. Not one person in the crowd missed the moment, for it was recorded for all to see on the giant-sized screen. As she

started to shake with shame, the good-natured crowd went
wild, applauding her, which helped her hold her nerve for
the final top note.

Thrust from his seat by a rocket-fuelled impulse to shield
and protect, Ethan was already shedding his jacket as he
stormed onto the pitch. By the time he reached
Savannah's side, the crowd had only just begun to take
in what had happened. Not so his target. Tears of frustration were pouring down her face as she struggled to re-
pin her dress. As he spoke to her and she looked at him
there was a moment, a potent and disturbing moment,
when she stared him straight in the eyes and he registered
something he hadn't felt for a long time, or maybe ever.
Without giving himself a chance to analyse the feeling,
he threw his jacket around her shoulders and led her away,
forcing the Italian tenor to launch into *Canto degli
Italiani*—or 'Song of the Italians', as the Italian national
anthem was known—somewhat sooner than expected.
    There was so much creamy flesh concealed beneath
his lightweight jacket it was throwing his brain synapses
out of sync. Unlike all the women he'd encountered to
date, this young Savannah Ross was having a profound
effect on his state of mind. He strode across the pitch with
his arm around her shoulders while she endeavoured to
keep in step and remain close, whilst not quite touching
him. As he took her past the stands the crowd went wild.
'Viva l'Orso!' the Italians cried, loving every minute of
it: 'hurrah for the Bear'. The England supporters cheered
him just as loudly. He wondered if this compliment was
to mark his chivalry or the fact that Ms Ross could hardly
conceal her hugely impressive bosom beneath a dress
that had burst its stitches. He hardly cared. His overrid-

ing thought was to get her out of the eyeline of every lustful male in the Stadio Flaminio, of whom there were far too many for his liking.

It crossed his mind that this incident would have to have happened in Italy, the land of romantic love and music, the home of passion and beauty. He had always possessed a dark sense of humour, and it amused him now to think that in his heart, the heart everyone was so mistakenly cheering for, there was only an arid desert and a single bitter note.

By the time Ethan had escorted Savannah into the shelter of the tunnel she was mortified. She felt ridiculously under-dressed in the company of a man noted for his *savoir faire*. Ethan Alexander was a ruthless, world-renowned tycoon, while she was an ordinary girl who didn't belong in the spotlight; a girl who wished, in a quite useless flash of longing, that Ethan could have met her on the farm where at least she knew what she was doing.

'Are you all right?' he asked her gruffly.

'Yes, thank you.'

He was holding on to her as if he thought she might fall over. Did he think her so pathetically weak? This was worse than her worst nightmare come true, and it was almost a relief when he turned away to make a call.

It couldn't be worse, Savannah concluded, taking in the wide, reassuring spread of Ethan's back. This was a very private man who had been thrust into the spotlight, thanks to her. No doubt he was calling for someone to come and take her away, nuisance that she was. She couldn't blame him. She had to be so much less in every way than he'd been expecting.

While he was so much more than she had expected…

Ethan Alexander in the flesh was a one-man power source of undiluted energy, a dynamo running on adrenalin and sex. At least that was what her vivid imagination was busy telling her, and she could hardly blame it for running riot. No television-screen or grainy newspaper-image had come close to conveying either Ethan's size or his compelling physical presence. And yet the most surprising shock of all was the way his lightest and most impersonal touch had scorched fireworks through every part of her. He'd only touched her elbow to help steer her, and had draped his jacket across her back, and yet that had been enough to hot-wire her arm and send sparks flying everywhere they shouldn't.

Her thoughts were interrupted by the young physio coming over to see if she could help. 'It wasn't your fault,' Savannah assured her, hoping Ethan could hear. She didn't want him blaming the young girl for Savannah's problems. 'It was my breathing,' she explained.

'What a problem we'd have had if you hadn't breathed!' The young physio shared a laugh with Savannah as she started pinning Savannah back into the dress. 'And I'm really glad you did breathe, because you were fantastic.'

Savannah had never been sure how to handle compliments. In her eyes she was just an ordinary girl with an extraordinary voice, and no manual had come with that voice to explain how to deal with the phenomenon that had followed. 'Thank you,' she said, spreading her hands wide in a modest gesture.

But the girl grabbed hold of them and shook them firmly. 'No,' she insisted, 'Don't you brush it off. You were fantastic. Everyone said so.'

Everyone? Savannah glanced at Ethan, who still had his back turned to her as he talked on the phone. She pulled his jacket close for comfort; it was warm and smelled faintly of sandalwood and spice. Tracing lapels that hung almost to her knees, she realised that even though Ethan's jacket was ten sizes too big for her it did little to preserve her modesty, and she hurriedly crossed her arms across her chest as he turned around.

'Okay, I've finished,' the physio reported. 'Though I doubt the pins on Ms Ross's dress will hold for long.'

'Right, let's go,' Ethan snapped, having thanked the girl.

'Go where?' Savannah held back nervously as the physio gave her a sympathetic look.

'Ms Ross, I know you've had a shock, but there are paparazzi crawling all over the building. Don't worry about your bag now,' Ethan said briskly when Savannah gazed down the tunnel. 'Your things will be sent on to you.'

'Sent where?'

'Just come with me, please.'

'Come with you *where*?' The thought of going anywhere with Ethan Alexander terrified her. He was such an imposing man, and an impatient one, but with all the paparazzi in the building the thought of not going with him terrified her even more.

'After you,' he said, giving her no option as he stood in a way that barred her getting past him.

'Where did you say we were going?'

'I didn't say.'

Savannah's nerve deserted her completely. She wasn't going anywhere with a man she didn't know, even if that man was her boss. 'You go. I'll be fine. I'll get a cab.'

'I brought you to Rome, and like it or not while you're here you're my responsibility.'

He didn't like it at all, she gathered, which left one simple question: did she want this recording contract or not?

She couldn't take the chance of losing it, Savannah realised. She hadn't come to Rome to sabotage her career. She might not like Ethan's manner, but she was here on his time. Plus, she didn't know Rome. If her only interest was getting home as quickly as possible, wasn't he her best hope?

She had to run to keep up with him, and then he stopped so suddenly she almost bumped into him. Looking up, Savannah found herself staring into a face that was even more cruelly scarred than she had remembered. Instead of recoiling, she registered a great well of feeling opening up inside her heart. It was almost as if something strong and primal was urging her to heal him, to press cream into those wounds, and to...*love him*?

This situation was definitely getting out of hand, Savannah concluded, pulling herself together, to find Ethan giving her an assessing look as if to warn her that just looking at him too closely was a dangerous game well out of her league. 'It's important we leave now,' he prompted as if she were some weakling he had been forced to babysit.

'I'm ready.' She held his gaze steadily. This was not a time to be proud. She didn't want to do battle with the paparazzi on her own, and she would be safer with Ethan. There were times when having a strong man at your side was a distinct advantage. But she wouldn't have him think her a fool either.

'After you.' Opening the door for her, he stood aside.

He looked more like a swarthy buccaneer than a businessman, and exuded the sort of earthy maleness she had always been drawn to. Her fantasies were full of pirates and cowboys, roughnecks and marines, though none of them had possessed lips as firm and sensual as Ethan's, and his hand in the small of her back was an incendiary device propelling her forward.

'What's wrong now?' he said impatiently when she stopped outside to shade her eyes.

'I was just looking for a taxi rank.' By far the safest option, she had decided.

'A taxi rank?' Ethan's voice was scathing. 'Do you want to attract more publicity? Don't worry, Ms Ross, you'll be quite safe with me.'

But would she? That was Savannah's cue for stepping back inside the stadium building. 'I'm sure someone will find the number of a cab company for me.'

'Please yourself.'

She couldn't have been more shocked when Ethan stormed ahead, letting the door swing in her face. Defiantly, she pushed it open again. 'You're leaving me?'

'That's what you want, isn't it?' he called back as he marched away. 'And as you don't need my help…'

'Just a minute.'

'You changed your mind?'

Savannah's heart lurched as Ethan turned to look at her. 'No, but.'

'But what?' He kept on walking.

'I need directions to the nearest taxi rank, and I thought you might know where I should look.' She had to run to keep up with him, which wasn't easy in high-heeled shoes, not to mention yards of taffeta winding itself like a malevolent red snake around her feet.

'Find someone else to help you.'

'Ethan, please!' She would have to swallow her pride if it meant saving her parents more embarrassment. 'Can you really get us out of here without the paparazzi seeing?'

He stopped and slowly turned around. 'Can I get us out of here?'

The look of male confidence blazing from his eyes was

at its purest. When she should be considering a thousand other things—like how long before the paparazzi found them, for example—a bolt of lust chose that moment to race down her spine. His eyes were the most beautiful eyes she'd ever seen, deep grey, with just a hint of duck-egg blue, and they had very white whites, as well as the most ridiculously long black lashes.

'I'm done waiting for you, Ms Ross.'

He was off again, but this time he grabbed her arm and took her with him. Savannah yelped with surprise. 'Where are we going?'

'To something that travels a lot faster than a taxi,' he grated without slowing down.

What did he mean—a helicopter? Of course. She should have known. Like all the super-rich, Ethan would hardly call a cab when he could fly home. 'Can we slow down just a bit?'

'And talk this through?' he scoffed without breaking stride. 'We can take all the time in the world if you want the paparazzi to find you.'

'You know I don't want that!' *Okay, no reason to worry*, Savannah told herself. They would fly straight to the airport in Ethan's helicopter, from where she'd fly home. Traffic snarl-ups were reserved for mere mortals like herself. In no time Ethan would be back in his seat at the stadium ready for the second half, while she returned to England and her nice, safe fantasies. Perfect.

Or at least it was until a door burst open and the press-hounds barrelled out. It only took one of them to catch sight of Ethan and Savannah for the whole pack to give chase.

'This way,' Ethan commanded, swinging Savannah in front of him. Opening a door, he thrust her through it and, slamming it shut, he shot the bolt home.

If she hadn't left her sensible sneakers in the tunnel she might have been able to run faster, Savannah fretted as Ethan took the stairs two at a time, but now the straps on her stratospheric heels were threatening to snap.

'Leave them!' he ordered as she bent down to take them off. 'Or, better still, snap those heels off.'

'Are you joking?'

'Take them off!' he roared.

'I'm going to keep them,' Savannah insisted stubbornly.

'Do what you like with them,' he said, snatching hold of her arm, half-lifting her to safety down another flight of steps. 'And hitch up your skirt while you're at it, before you trip over it,' he said, checking outside the next door before rushing her out into the open air again. 'Your skirt—hitch it up!'

Hitch it up? The photographers would surely be on them in moments, and when that happened she didn't want to look like a...

'Do it!'

'I'm doing it!' she yelled, startled into action. But she wouldn't ruin the shoes her mother had bought her. Or Madame's dress. Slipping off her high-heeled sandals as quickly as she could, Savannah bundled up the gown, noting she barely reached Ethan's shoulder now. Also noting he barely seemed to notice her naked legs, which shouldn't bother her, but for some reason did.

'Come on,' he rapped impatiently, still averting his gaze. 'There's no time to lose.' Taking her arm, he urged her on.

Savannah was totally incapable of speech by the time they'd crossed the car park. Yet still Ethan was merciless. 'There's no time for that,' he assured her when she rested with her hands on her knees to catch her breath.

Straightening up, she stared at him. She didn't know

this man. She didn't know anything about him, other than the fact that his reputation was well deserved. The Bear was a dark and formidable man, whom she found incredibly intimidating. And she was going who knew where with him. 'You still haven't told me where we're going.'

'There's no time!'

'But you do have a helicopter waiting?'

'A helicopter?' Ethan glanced towards the roof where the helipad was situated.

He had a helicopter there, all right, she could see the logo of a bear on the tail. She could also see the scrum of photographers gathered round it.

'A useful distraction,' Ethan told her with satisfaction.

A red herring, Savannah realised, to put the paparazzi off the trail. 'So what now?'

'Now you can sit,' he promised, dangling a set of keys in front of her face.

Ah…She relaxed a little at the thought that life was about to take on a more regular beat. She should have known Ethan would have a car here. His driver would no doubt take them straight to the airport, where the helicopter would meet him and she would fly home. She was guilty of overreacting again. Ethan was entitled to his privacy. He'd taken her out of reach of the paparazzi and saved her and her parents any further humiliation. She should be grateful to him. But she still felt a little apprehensive.

CHAPTER THREE

EVEN with the knowledge that comfort was only a few footsteps away, Savannah reminded herself that this was not one of her fantasies and Ethan was no fairy-tale hero. He was a cold, hard man who inhabited a world far beyond the safety curtain of a theatre, and as such she should be treating him with a lot more reserve and more caution than the type of men she was used to mixing with.

'Put this on.'

She recoiled as he thrust something at her, and then she stared at it in bewilderment. 'What's this?'

'A helmet,' he said with that ironic tone again. 'Put it on.' When she didn't respond right away. he gave it a little shake for emphasis.

It was only then she noticed the big, black motorbike parked up behind him and laughed nervously. 'You're not serious, I hope?'

'Why shouldn't I be serious?' Ethan frowned. Dipping his head, he demanded, 'You're not frightened of riding a bike, are you?'

'Of course not,' Savannah protested, swallowing hard as she straightened up. Was she frightened of sitting on a big, black, vibrating machine pressed up close to Ethan?

'If you have any better suggestions, Ms Ross…?'

Watching Ethan settle a formidable-looking helmet on his thick, wavy hair, she mutely shook her head.

'Well?' he said, swinging one hard-muscled thigh over the bike. 'Would you care to join me, or shall I leave you here?'

She was still staring at the tightly packed jeans settled comfortably into the centre of the saddle, Savannah realised. 'No…no,' she repeated more firmly. 'I'm coming with you.' Remembering the door incident, she already knew he took no prisoners. Holding up her skirt, she hopped, struggled, and finally managed to yank her leg over the back of the bike—which wasn't easy without touching him.

'Helmet?'

As Ethan turned to look at her, Savannah thought his eyes were darker than ever through the open visor—a reflection of his black helmet, she told herself, trying not to notice the thick, glossy waves of bitter-chocolate hair that had escaped and fallen over the scars on his forehead. But those scars were still there, like the dark side of Ethan behind the superficial glamour of a fiercely good-looking man. Her stomach flipped as she wondered how many more layers there were to him, and what he was really thinking behind those gun-metal-grey eyes.

'Helmet,' he rapped impatiently.

Startled out of her dreams, she started fumbling frantically with it.

'Let me,' he offered.

This was the closest they'd been since the stadium, and as Ethan handled the catch he held her gaze. In the few seconds it took him to complete the task every part of her had been subjected to his energy, which left her thrumming with awareness. And he hadn't even started the engine yet, Savannah reminded herself as a door banged open and a dozen or so photographers piled out. Snapping his own visor into position, Ethan swung away from her and stamped the powerful machine into life. 'Hang on.'

There was barely time to register that instruction before he released the brake, gunned the engine, and they roared off like a rocket.

Propelled by terror, Savannah flung her arms around Ethan, clinging to as much of him as she could. Forced to press her cheek against his crisp blue shirt, she kept her eyes shut, trusting him to get them out of this. But as the bike gained speed something remarkable happened. Maybe it was the persistent throb of the engine, or the feel of Ethan's muscular back against her face—or maybe it was simply the fact that she had a real-life hunk beneath her hands instead of one of her disappointing fantasies— but Savannah felt the tension ebb away and began to enjoy herself. She was enjoying travelling at what felt like the speed of sound, and not in a straight line either. Because this wasn't just the ride of her life, Savannah concluded, smiling a secret smile, but the closest to sex she'd ever come.

As Ethan raced the bike between the ranks of parked cars she was pleased to discover how soon she became used to leaning this way and that to help him balance. She could get used to this, Savannah decided, sucking in her first full and steady breath since climbing on board. She felt so safe with Ethan. He made her feel safe. His touch was sure, his judgement was sound, and his strength could only be an asset in any situation. There was something altogether reassuring about being with him, she concluded happily.

When she wasn't being terrified by him, her sober self chimed in.

Ignoring these internal reservations, she went with the excitement of the moment—not that she needed an excuse to press her face against Ethan's back. As she inhaled the intoxicating cocktail of sunshine, washing powder and warm, clean man, she decided that just for once she was going to keep her sensible self at bay and ride this baby like a biker chick.

Ethan was forced to slow the bike as he engaged with the heavy traffic approaching Rome, and Savannah took this opportunity to do some subtle finger-mapping. She reckoned she had only a few seconds before Ethan's attention would be back on the bike and his passenger, and she intended to make the most of them. He felt like warm steel beneath her fingertips, and she could detect the shift of muscle beneath his shirt. She smiled against his back, unseen and secure. She felt so tiny next to him, which made her wonder what such a powerful man could teach her, locking these erotic reveries away in record time when he gunned the engine and turned sharp right.

The bike banked dramatically as they approached the Risorgimento Bridge spanning the river Tiber, forcing Savannah to lean over at such an angle her knee was almost brushing the road. As she did so she realised it was the first time she had ever put her trust in someone outside her close-knit family. But with the Roman sun on her face, and the excitement of the day, clinging on to a red-hot man didn't seem like such a bad option, she told herself wryly. In fact, who would travel by helicopter, given an alternative like this?

She was feeling so confident by the time Ethan levelled

up the bike again, she even turned around to see if they were being followed.

'I thought I told you to sit still.'

Savannah nearly jumped off the bike with fright, hearing Ethan's voice barking at her through some sort of headphone in her helmet.

'Hold on,' he repeated harshly.

'I am holding on,' she shouted back.

As if she needed an excuse.

They took another right and headed back up the river the way they'd come, only on the opposite side of the Tiber. Ethan slowed the bike when they reached the Piazalle Maresciallo Giardino where there was another bridge and, moored under it, a powerboat...

No.

No!

Savannah shook her head, refusing to believe the evidence of her own eyes. This couldn't possibly be the next stage of their journey. Or was that one of the reasons Ethan had been making that call back at the stadium, to line everything up?

'Come on,' he rapped, shaking her out of her confusion the moment they parked up.

As she fumbled with the clasp Ethan lifted her visor and removed the helmet for her. As his fingers brushed her face she trembled. Staring into his eyes, she thought it another of those moments where fantasy collided with reality. But was Ethan really looking at her differently, as if she might be more than just a package he was delivering to the airport? The suspicion that he might be seeing her for the first time as a woman was a disturbing thought, and so she turned away to busy herself with the pretence of straightening out her ruined hair. She still had her precious high-heels dangling from her wrist like a bracelet, which turned her thoughts to her mother and what she would make of this situation. Her mother was a stand-up woman and would make the most of it, Savannah concluded, as would she.

'Are you thinking of joining me any time today?'

She looked up to find Ethan already on board the boat, preparing to cast off. He leaned over the side to call to her, 'Get up here, or I'll come and get you!'

Would you? crossed her mind. Brushing the momentary weakness aside, she called back, 'Wait for me.'

'Not for long,' he assured her. 'You're not frightened of a little mud, are you?' he added, taunting her as she teetered down the embankment.

Frightened of a little mud? He clearly hadn't seen their farmyard recently. 'What sort of wet lettuce do you think I am?'

'You'd prefer me not to answer that.'

'I'm not all sequins and feathers, you know!' She kicked the hem of her gown away with one dirty foot for emphasis.

'You don't say.' Ethan's tone was scathing, and then she noticed their chins were sticking out at the same combative angle and quickly pulled hers in again.

'There is an element of urgency to this. Paparazzi?' Ethan reminded her in a voice that could have descaled a kettle.

And then car horns started up behind her. She was providing some unexpected entertainment for the male drivers of Rome, who were slowing their vehicles to whistle and shout comments at her. They must think she was still in evening dress after a wild night out with an even wilder man, Savannah realised self-consciously. A man who was threatening to make good on his promise to come and get her, she also realised, detecting movement in her peripheral vision. 'Stay back,' she warned Ethan as he took a step towards her. 'I don't need your help.'

It was a relief to see him lift his hands up, palms flat in an attitude of surrender. She had enough to do picking her way across the splintery walkway without worrying about what Ethan might do.

It was just a shame she missed his ironic stare. The next thing she knew she was several feet off the ground travelling at speed towards the boat. 'Put me down!'

Ethan ignored her. 'I can't live life at your pace. young lady. If you stay around me much longer, you'll have to learn to tick a lot faster.'

She had no intention of 'staying around' him a moment longer than she had to, Savannah determined. But, pressed against Ethan's firm, warm body, a body that rippled with hard, toned muscle… 'Please put me down,' she murmured, hoping he wouldn't hear.

Ethan didn't react either way. He didn't slow his pace until they were onboard, when he lowered her onto the deck. Having done this, he surveyed her sternly. 'The race is still on,' he said, folding massive arms across his chest. 'And I have no intention of giving up, or of allowing anyone to hold me back. Is that clear?'

'Crystal.'

'Good.'

Savannah smoothed her palms down her arms where Ethan's hand prints were still branded.

'Well, Ms Ross, shall we take this powerboat on the river?'

'Whatever it takes,' she agreed, watching Ethan move to straddle the space between the shore and the boat.

'I'm going to free the mooring ropes,' he explained, springing onto the shore. 'Can you catch a rope?'

Could she catch a rope? He really did think she was completely useless, Savannah thought, huffing with frustration. Ethan had got her so wrong. 'I might have smaller hands than you, but I still have opposing thumbs.'

Was that a smile? Too late to tell, as Ethan had already turned away.

'In that case, catch this.'

He turned back to her so fast she almost dropped the rope. It was heavier than she had imagined and she stumbled drunkenly under the weight of it.

'All right?' Ethan demanded as he sprang back on board.

'Absolutely fine,' she lied. Summoning her last reserves of strength, she hoisted it up to brandish it at him.

'Now coil it up,' he instructed, pointing to where she should place it when she'd done so.

'Okay.' She could do this. Quite honestly, she enjoyed the feel of the rough rope beneath her fingers—and enjoyed the look of grudging admiration on Ethan's face even more. But she needed to even the playing field. Ethan was dressed appropriately for taking a powerboat down the river. She was dressed, but barely. 'Do you have a jumper, or something I could borrow?'

Ethan made a humming sound as he looked her over. 'I see your point.'

Savannah felt heat rise to her cheeks and depart southwards.

'I'll see what I can do for you,' Ethan offered, brushing past her on his way across the deck. 'I must have an old shirt stowed here somewhere…'

Her nipples responded with indecent eagerness to this

brief contact with him, just as a fresh flurry of car horns started up on shore. Who could blame the drivers? Savannah thought. The sight of a decidedly scruffy girl in an ill-fitting evening dress onboard a fabulous powerboat in the middle of the afternoon with a clearly influential man of some considerable means would naturally cause a sensation in Rome. But why couldn't Ethan notice her?

'What's wrong?' he said when he straightened up, and then his stare swept the line of traffic. One steely look from him was all it took for the cars to speed up again. 'Will this do?' he said, turning back to Savannah. He thrust a scrunched-up nondescript bundle at her.

The shirt was maybe twenty sizes too large, Savannah saw as she shook it out, but in the absence of anything else to wear she'd have to go with it. Plus it held the faint but unmistakeable scent of Ethan's cologne. 'It's absolutely perfect. Thank you.' Slipping it on, she realised it brushed her calves, but at least she was decent. She pulled the shirt close and, inhaling Ethan's scent deeply, gave a smile of true contentment, the first she'd unleashed that day.

He was stunned by the sight of Savannah wearing his shirt. She looked…adorable. She looked, in fact, as he imagined she might look if they had just been to bed together. Her hair was mostly hanging loose now, and the make-up she'd worn for her appearance on the pitch was smudged, which made her eyes seem huge in her heart-shaped face, and her lips appeared bruised as if he'd kissed them for hours. His shirt drowned her, of course, but knowing what was underneath didn't help his equilibrium any. Hard to believe he had looked at her properly, critically, for the first time just a few moments ago when she'd asked for the shirt. Nothing on earth would have induced him to stare at her out on the pitch where she'd been at such a disadvantage. But now? Now he couldn't take his eyes off her fuller figure.

Savannah tensed guiltily as unexpectedly Ethan's gaze warmed. What was he thinking—that she was a fat mess? A nuisance? As sophisticated as a sheep? Before her imagination could take her any further, she took her seat. 'I'm on it,' she assured Ethan when he glanced at the harness.

She couldn't do the darn thing up. And now Ethan was giving her the type of superior male appraisal that got right up her nose.

'I don't seem to have the knack,' she admitted with frustration. Maybe because her hands were shaking with nerves at being in such close proximity to Ethan.

'Would you like me to fasten it for you?' Ethan offered with studied politeness.

As he leaned over to secure the catch for her, Savannah felt like she was playing with fire. Ethan's hair was so thick and glossy she longed to run her fingers through it. And he smelled so good. His touch was so sure, and so…disappointingly fast. She looked down. The clasp was securely fastened. 'Is that it?'

'Would you like there to be something more?'

As he asked the question Savannah thought Ethan's stare to be disturbingly direct. 'No, thank you,' she told him primly, turning away on the pretence of tossing her tangled hair out of her eyes. But even as she was doing that Ethan was lifting his overlarge shirt onto her shoulders from where it had slipped.

'Are you sure you're warm enough?' he asked gruffly. 'Only it can be cold out on the river.'

Or hot to sizzling. 'I'll be fine, thank you.' Each tiny hair on the back of her neck had stood to attention at his touch, and it was a real effort not to notice that Ethan had the sexiest mouth she had ever seen. She would have to make sure she stared unswervingly ahead for the rest of the boat ride.

CHAPTER FOUR

'Now what are you doing?' Ethan demanded. He had just opened up the throttle, and as the boat surged forward it pitched and yawed; Savannah had chosen that very moment to shed her harness, which forced him to throttle back.

'I'm calling my parents.'

'Calling your—?' He was lost for words. 'Not now!' he roared back at her above the scream of the boat's engine.

'They'll be worried about me.'

This was a concept so alien to him it took him a moment to respond. 'Sit down, Savannah, and buckle up.' He spoke with far more restraint than he felt and, after congratulating himself on that restraint, he conceded in the loud voice needed to crest the engines, 'You can speak to them later.'

She reluctantly agreed, but he detected anxiety in her tone. He also detected the same desire to protect Savannah he'd felt out on the pitch, except now it had grown. His intention to remain distant and aloof, because she was young and innocent and he was not, was dead in the water. There was too much feminine warmth too close. 'I'll speak to them,' he said, wanting to reassure her.

Savannah was right, he conceded, her parents must be

worried about her, having seen everything unfold on television. 'You can speak to them after I do,' he said. 'But for now *sit down*.' And on this there could be no compromise.

Even Savannah couldn't defy that tone of voice, and he made sure she was securely fastened in before picking up speed again. It amused him to see she had pushed back the sleeves on his overly large shirt and pulled it tightly around her legs, as if she felt the need to hide every bit of naked flesh from him. He supposed he could see her point of view. They were diametrically opposed on the gender scale. He was all man and she was a distraction. Fixing his attention to the river, he thrust the throttles forward.

'This is wonderful!' she exclaimed excitedly as the powerboat picked up speed and the prow lifted from the water.

It pleased him to see her looking so relaxed, and he even allowed himself a small smile as he remembered her jibe about opposing thumbs. There was a lot more to Ms Ross than the circumstance of their first meeting might have led him to suppose.

What exactly that might be was for some other man to discover, though, because this was strictly a taxi service to get Savannah out of harm's way as fast as he could.

Oh, yes, it was, he argued with his unusually quarrelsome inner voice.

She was only here because she had no other option, Savannah reassured herself as the powerboat zoomed along the river. She was glad she'd been able to catch the rope and prove to Ethan she wasn't completely helpless—after the debacle at the stadium she certainly needed something to go right, but she still had some way to go. She cupped her ear as he said something to her. It was so hard to hear anything above the rhythmical pounding of the boat.

'You're not feeling seasick, are you?'

'On the river?' she yelled back. This riposte earned her a wry look from Ethan that made her cheeks flame. He might be stern and grim, but she still thought he had the most fantastic eyes she had ever seen, and there was some humour in there somewhere. It was up to her to dig it out. But for now... To escape further scrutiny, she dipped her head to secure the strap on her sandals.

'You can't put those on here.'

Savannah's head shot up. 'But my feet are filthy. Surely you don't want them soiling your pristine deck?'

'I don't want them anywhere near me,' Ethan assured her, which for some reason made Savannah picture her naked feet rubbing the length of Ethan's muscular thighs and writhing limbs entwined on cool, crisp sheets.

Swallowing hard, she quickly composed herself whilst tucking her feet safely away beneath the seat. Such a relief she had Ethan's shirt to wrap around her; Madame's gown was split to kingdom come, and what little modesty she had left she had every intention of hanging on to.

But as the river rushed past the side of the boat, and Savannah thought about the flicker of humour she'd seen in Ethan's eyes, modesty began to feel like a handicap. If only she knew how to flirt...

Flirt? Fortunately, she wouldn't be given a chance. Savannah's sensible inner self breathed a sigh of relief as at that moment Ethan looked behind them. He must think they were still being followed, Savannah reasoned. She did too. The paparazzi would hardly have given up the chase. But she felt safe with Ethan at the helm. With his sleeves rolled back, revealing hard-muscled and tanned forearms, he gave her confidence—and inner flutters too. In fact the sight of these powerful arms was apparently connected to a cord that ran from her dry throat to a place it was safer not to think about.

Had she lost her grip on reality altogether?

With every mile they travelled she was moving further and further away from everything that was safe and familiar into a shadowy world inhabited by a man she hardly knew. As the boat spewed out a plume of glittering foam behind them, Savannah couldn't shake the feeling she was racing into danger, and at breakneck speed.

There were many things he could do without in life, and of all them this fluffy thing in the oversized shirt was top of his list—though Savannah could be feisty. She had a stinging retort, for example, should she wish to use it. Far from that being a negative, he found it very much in her favour. She was also a real family girl, and, given that her parents would have undoubtedly seen everything unfolding live on television in their front room she had kept a cool head and thought not of herself but of them. A quick glance revealed her checking her feet. No doubt her pedicure was ruined. She was the smoothest, most pampered and perfect person he'd ever met, and possessed the type of wholesomeness that could only be damaged by him.

Feeling his interest, she looked up. He should be glad they couldn't hold a conversation above the thundering of the hull on the water. He had no small talk for her; he'd lived alone too long. His passion for rugby, one of the roughest contact-sports known to man, defined him. The majority of his business dealings were conducted on construction sites, where he loved nothing more than getting his hands dirty.

He was well named the Bear, and the contrast between him and Savannah was so extreme it was almost laughable; only the music they both loved so much provided a tenuous link between them. Forced to wrench the wheel to avoid some children fooling around in a dinghy, he was surprised at the way his body reacted when Savannah grabbed hold of him to steady herself.

'Sorry!' she exclaimed, snatching her hand away as if he'd burned her.

He was the one who'd been burned. Savannah was playing havoc with his slumbering libido and, instead of shouting at her to sit down, he found himself slowing the boat to check that she was all right.

'I am now,' she assured him, and then they both turned around to make sure the children were okay.

As their eyes briefly clashed he was conscious of the ingenuous quality of her gaze. It warmed him and he lusted after more of that feeling. He needed innocence around him. And yet he could only sully it, he reminded himself. But he hadn't meant to frighten her, and it didn't hurt to take a moment to reassure her now.

'You're not such a baddy, are you?' she said to his surprise.

In spite of his self-control his lips twitched as he shrugged. A *baddy*? He had to curb the urge to smile. He'd shut himself off from all that was soft and feminine for too long. Living life by his own very masculine rules and preferences, he hadn't been called upon to take anyone else's feelings into account for quite some time. And a woman like Savannah's? Never. 'A baddy,' he repeated. 'I've never been called that before.'

It was as if she saw him differently from everyone else on the planet. He smiled. He couldn't help himself. Paying close attention to the river, he didn't look at her, but he knew that she was smiling too.

No sooner had he begun to soften towards Savannah than he reverted to coldly examining the facts. Did he need this sort of distraction in his life? Savannah was very young and had a lot of growing up to do. Did he want the attention of the world centred on him, when he'd success-fully avoided publicity for so long? He'd gone to the match with the sole intention of supporting his friends in the England squad, and it was them who should be getting the attention, not him. He felt a stab of something repre-hensible, and recognised it as envy. The days when he'd hoped to play rugby for England weren't so far away, but the past could never be recaptured. He had learned to adapt and change direction since then; he'd moved on. But the facts remained: the injuries he'd sustained during a prolonged beating by a gang of thugs had meant the club doctors had been unable to sign the insurance documents he needed to play his part in the professional game. And so his career had come to an abrupt and unwanted end.

But none of this was Savannah's fault. He might be drawn to her, but he wouldn't taint her with his darkness. He would fight the attraction he felt for her. Some might say he needed a woman like Savannah to soften him, but he knew that the last thing Savannah needed in her life was a man like him.

'I'm sorry you've missed the match, Ethan.'

The river was quieter here and he cut the engines. 'Don't worry about it. I'll watch the replay on television later.'

'But you can't detect the scent of excitement on a screen,' she said with concern.

Or feel the ravages of failure, the blaze of triumph… Yes, he knew that, but he was surprised Savannah did. 'It's no big deal.'

'Yes it is,' she said, pulling a face that made him think

how pretty she was. 'You'd be there now if it wasn't for me.' Frowning with concern, she began plucking threads from his ancient shirt.

He didn't prolong the exchange. He didn't like people getting close to him. He was a bear licking his wounds in the shadows, full of unresolved conflict and bitterness, and chose not to inflict himself on anyone—least of all an innocent young girl like Savannah.

'Watching England play must be both a passion and a torment for you.'

Why wouldn't she let it rest?

'Perhaps,' he agreed, accepting she meant no harm by these comments and was only trying to make conversation. It was public knowledge that the damage to his spine had ended his career. Lifting he could do, running he could do, but to risk another knock, another blow...

'You could let me off here, if it's quicker for you.'

He followed her gaze to a nearby landing stage. 'I could let you swim to the far bank,' he offered dryly. 'That might save some time.'

Her expression lifted, which pleased him. He didn't want to intimidate her, though his appearance must have done that already. Mooring up and calling a cab to take her to the airport was what he should do. He should let her go.

But the decision was taken out of his hands by the sound of rotor blades. The paparazzi's helicopter was still some way off, but it was approaching fast. There was no time to do anything more than hit the throttle and tell Savannah to hold on.

'They've found us?' she shouted above the roar of the engines.

Oh, yes. The race was back on. And no way was he going to let them catch her. 'Yes, they've found us,' he confirmed grimly. 'Sit tight.'

The spray was in her hair, her eyes, and her knuckles had turned white with holding on. If she'd been nervous before, she was terrified now. It was one thing showing a brave face to the world when things were going well, but the black, menacing shadow of the paparazzi helicopter would soon beam a travesty of the true situation around the world. Adding fuel to the paparazzi's fire, she was forced to cling to Ethan as he pushed the powerboat to its limits, because he was the only stable element in a world that was tipping and yawing as the currents played bat and ball with their hull.

Nothing had gone right for Ethan since she'd turned up in Rome, Savannah thought guiltily, and though he hardly knew her he had insisted on fighting her corner in spite of the personal cost to him. He must be wondering what he'd done to deserve such aggravation!

CHAPTER FIVE

As a surge of water threw the delicately balanced boat off kilter, Ethan fastened his arm protectively around Savannah's shoulders. At first she tensed, but then slowly relaxed. Ethan had no idea how profoundly his protective instinct affected her. Coming from a man as cold as he was, his smallest touch bore the intensity of a kiss. She could get used to this physical closeness all too easily. But they would soon reach the airport, she would fly home, and she would be nothing more than a tiresome memory to him. But at least the helicopter was wheeling away. 'Fuel shortage?' she suggested hopefully.

'I think you're being a little over-optimistic,' Ethan said as he powered back the engines. 'My best guess is they got the photographs they came for and their work is done.'

'How can you be so calm about it? Don't you care?'

'I don't waste time regretting things that can't be changed.'

'But they breached your privacy. Won't you make some sort of protest?'

Her heart jolted to see Ethan's lips tug in a smile. 'I hope you're not suggesting I should try to curb the freedom of the press?'

'Of course not, but.'

'But?' he pressed.

'Well, I just can't roll over.'

'You don't have to,' he pointed out. 'It's happened and I'll deal with it.'

'Okay, well, my parents are going to be devastated. What if the press are there right now, hammering on their door? Ethan, I have to call them.'

He couldn't imagine anyone else on earth in this predicament thinking of placing an international call, but he was fast learning that Savannah's first thought was always for others, and he envied the loving relationship she obviously enjoyed with her parents and would never stand in the way of it. 'I'll speak to them first to reassure them, and then you can speak,' he suggested, warming to her.

'Would you really do that?'

Her relief made him think he should have done it sooner. 'Number?'

As she recited it he punched it in to his mobile phone, and it occurred to him that Savannah must have no idea how lucky she was to have a loving family.

'You didn't have to do that,' she said several minutes later when she had finished speaking to her mother.

'I wanted to,' he admitted. 'It was the right thing to do,' he added sternly when Savannah's face softened into a smile.

'It was very kind of you.'

'It was nothing,' he argued, turning his attention back to sailing the boat. 'All I did was point out that my legal team will handle any press intrusion, and reassure your parents that they mustn't worry because you were safe with me.'

'You gave them your private number.'

'How else are they supposed to call me?'

'Well, thank you,' she said sincerely.

'Your mother seemed reassured,' he said, unbending a little. His reward was to see Savannah's face softening into a smile.

Her mother had been reassured, Savannah reflected with relief. Her romantic mother had always been a sucker for a strong man, though she preferred them safely corralled on the cover of a book or on a screen at the cinema, and kept a well-trained beta hero at home. She wondered if her mother would be quite so reassured if she could see Ethan in the flesh.

'I have another call to make,' Ethan told her, turning away.

As Ethan stood in profile his scars were cruelly exposed, and it appalled her to think one person could do that to another. But surely it couldn't have been one person—it had to have been more—a gang, maybe? She'd felt a fraction of Ethan's strength today and he was bigger, stronger and fitter than most men. What kamikaze group of yobs would have dared to take him on?

Trained yobs—professional thugs, truly evil men— was the only conclusion she could possibly come to. No casual attack could result in such serious injuries. But who would pay such men to beat Ethan so severely he'd nearly lost his life and *had* lost his sporting career? Professional rugby might be a highly competitive sport, but it was hardly a killing ground.

As Ethan finished his call and stowed the phone, turning the wheel to negotiate a bend in the river, Savannah was wondering if the person behind Ethan's beating also accounted for the darkness in his eyes. If so Ethan carried far more scars than were visible to the naked eye. 'Are we going to the airport?' she said, noticing he was steering the boat towards a tributary.

'To the airport first, and then to my place in Tuscany—just until the heat dies down.'

'To Tuscany?' She was feeling more out of her depth than ever.

'Unless you'd prefer me to leave you to the mercy of the press?'

Savannah's heart turned over as Ethan looked at her. How childish he must think her. Women would scratch each other's eyes out for the chance to be with Ethan like this, and yet she had sounded so apprehensive at the prospect of staying with him. 'I don't want to be left to that pack of hounds,' she confessed. 'But I've put you out so much already.'

'So a little more trouble won't hurt me,' Ethan reassured her dryly.

Maybe his lack of enthusiasm didn't match up with her fantasies, but what Ethan had suggested was a sensible solution. And his place in Tuscany sounded so romantic—such a pity it would be wasted on them. 'Are you sure it wouldn't be easier for you if I just fly home?'

'If you do that you won't be able to take advantage of the security I can provide. It would take me quite some time to get the same level of protection set up for you in England, which is why I've made some arrangements for your parents.'

'Arrangements? What arrangements?' Savannah interrupted anxiously.

'I decided a cruise would take them well out of the range of prying eyes.'

'A cruise?' She gasped. 'Are you serious?'

'Why wouldn't I be serious?'

'You mean you booked a holiday for them?'

'It's the best solution I could come up with,' he said, as if booking fabulously expensive trips was nothing unusual for him.

Savannah couldn't stop smiling. 'You have no idea what this will mean to them. I can't remember the last time they went away—or even if they ever have been away from the farm.'

'The farm?'

'I live on a farm.' She shook her head, full of excitement. 'You must have seen my address on file?'

'Lots of addresses have the word "farm" in them. It doesn't mean a thing.'

'Well, in this instance it means a great deal,' she assured him, turning serious. Savannah's voice had dropped and emotion hung like a curtain between them, a curtain Ethan swiftly brushed aside.

'Well, I'm pleased I've made the appropriate arrangements.'

'Oh, you have,' Savannah said softly, thinking of all the times she'd wished she could have sent her exhausted parents away for a break, but she had never had the money to do so. Their grief when they'd lost their herd of dairy cows to disease had exacted a terrible toll, and they'd only survived it thanks to the support of the wonderful people who worked alongside them. Those same people would stand in for them now, allowing them to take the holiday they deserved.

'You've no idea what you've done for them,' Savannah assured Ethan.

He brushed off her thanks, as Savannah had known he would. But because of his generosity she thought he deserved to be wholly in the picture, and so she told him how her parents had stood by and watched their whole herd being slaughtered—animals they'd known by name.

'That must have cost you all dearly,' he observed, looking at her closely. 'And not just in financial terms.'

It was a rare moment between them, but Ethan scarcely gave her a chance to enjoy it before switching back to practicalities. He treated emotion like an enemy that must be fought off at every turn, Savannah thought as Ethan told her that her bags would probably arrive at the *palazzo* before she did.

'Just a minute,' she said, interrupting him. 'Did you say "the *palazzo*"?' Of all the day's surprises, this was the biggest. Ethan had just turned all her points of reference on their head. As far as Savannah was concerned, a *palazzo* was somewhere people who existed on another planet lived.

'There are a lot of *palazzos* in Tuscany,' Ethan explained, as if it were nothing, but as Savannah continued to stare incredulously at him he finally admitted, 'Okay, so I've got a very nice place in Tuscany.'

'You're a very lucky man,' she told him frankly.

In the light of what Savannah had just told him about her parents' hardships, he had no doubt that was true. At least they'd be able to put plenty of space between each other at the *palazzo*, he reminded himself thankfully.

'Tell me about your *palazzo*.'

Finding he was staring at her lips as she spoke, he turned away. 'Later,' he said, relieved to see his driver waiting exactly where he had asked him to, by the landing stage. He waved to the man as he cut the engines and allowed the powerboat to glide into shore. 'We'll disembark first, and then I'll tell you more about it when we're on my jet.'

But she was back on the ground and in the back of a second limousine before Ethan turned to answer her questions.

'The name of the *palazzo*?' he resumed, leaning over from the front seat where he sat next to the driver. 'The Palazzo dei Tramonti Dorati.'

'That's quite a name.' Savannah laughed as she tried to say it, stumbling over the unfamiliar Italian words, acutely conscious as she did so that Ethan was watching her lips move.

'Not bad,' he said, congratulating her on her accent.

'What does it mean?' Savannah found that she badly wanted to hold Ethan's attention.

'It means "the Palace of the Golden Sunset".'

He hadn't meant to enter into conversation with her, but how could he not when she glowed with pleasure at the smallest thing? It reminded him, of course, of how very young she was, but even so he couldn't subdue the urge to tell her about a home he loved above all his others.

'It sounds so romantic!' she exclaimed, her eyes turning dreamy.

'Yes, it's a very old and very beautiful building.' He knew he was being drawn in, but he would never forget his first sight of the *palazzo*, and he'd had no one to share it with before. 'The towers glow rose-pink at sunset,' he explained, though he left out the emotional angle, which had entailed a longing to own the ancient *palazzo* that had come from the depths of his soul.

'The *palazzo* is located in a glorious valley blessed with sunlight, and the medieval village surrounding it is inhabited by wonderful people who appreciate the simple things in life.' And who had taken him to their heart, he remembered with gratitude. As he tried to convey something of this passion to Savannah without becoming overly sentimental, she remained silent and alert, as if what he didn't say told her everything she needed to know.

She confirmed this, saying softly when he had finished, 'You're even luckier than I thought.'

'Yes, well…' He left the statement hanging, feeling he'd gone too far. He wasn't a man to brag about his possessions, or even mention them.

Ethan was full of surprises. His sensitivity was obvious once he started talking about the *palazzo*. He flew planes, he rode bikes, he drove powerboats, and he had a perfect command of the Italian language. The thought that he did everything well and was capable of such passion sent a frisson of arousal shimmering through her.

Which she would put a stop to right away! Savannah's sensible inner voice commanded. It was one thing to fantasise about sexual encounters with Ethan, but quite another to consider the reality of it when she was saving her virginity for some sensible, 'steady Eddie' type of bloke, and then only when they were married.

'Are you too warm?' Ethan asked, misreading the flush that rose to her cheeks as she moved restlessly on the seat. 'I can easily adjust the temperature for you.'

Savannah bit her lip to hide her smile.

'What's so funny?' he demanded suspiciously.

What was so funny? Ethan was the man most women had voted to go to bed with, and she was the woman most men had decided not to go to bed with—that was funny, wasn't it?

'I asked you a question, Savannah.'

The easy atmosphere that had so briefly existed between them had suddenly gained an edge.

'Is it my scars?' he pressed. 'Do they make you nervous?'

Ethan had read her all wrong, Savannah realised. He was so far off the mark, she shook her head in shock. 'Of course they don't.' It was no use, because Ethan wasn't listening.

'Is that why you're trying so hard not to laugh?' he demanded.

'I've told you, no!' She held his gaze. There must be no doubt over this. She would be the first to admit she was overawed by Ethan, and that he even frightened her a little, but those feelings were all tied up in his worldliness contrasted with her own inexperienced sexual-self, and had not the slightest connection with his scars. If he thought she was shallow enough to be intimidated by them... Savannah shook her head with disgust at the thought. As far as she was concerned, Ethan's terrible scars were just a reminder that even the strongest tree could be felled. 'I see the man, not the scars,' she told him bluntly.

In the confines of the limousine his short, disbelieving laugh sounded cruel and hard.

That had to come from some memory in his past, Savannah reassured herself, refusing to rise to the bait. Sometimes it was better to say nothing, she was learning, and to persuade Ethan she was more than the fluffy girl he thought her would take action, not words. She had been raised on a working farm and knew the value of hard work. She was used to getting her hands dirty and wasn't frightened of much.

Just as well, Savannah reflected as Ethan turned away with a face like thunder to continue his conversation with the driver, because there was nothing easy about Ethan Alexander. But whatever Ethan's opinion of her, she would stand up for herself. Perhaps he had learned that much about her. If nothing else this journey was giving them both the opportunity to learn a little more about each other. What she'd learned might not be reassuring, but it hadn't put her off Ethan either—in fact, quite the reverse.

CHAPTER SIX

As THEY approached the end of the journey they sat in silence, and Ethan could sense Savannah's unease. For all her excitement at the thought of seeing his *palazzo*, she was wondering what she had got herself into. He had always been intuitive. His mother had told him he was keenly tuned, close to the earth and all its mystery. She'd told him that before the crystal sphere she'd kept next to her bed told her to marry for the fourth time, apparently. At seven years old he had begged her not to do it, believing it would be a disastrous move for his mother and for himself. She had ignored him and the marriage had been a disaster. So much for his mother's belief in his special powers. The beatings had begun the day his new 'daddy' had arrived back from their honeymoon. He'd gone away to school that September, and had been the only boy in his class relieved to be living away from home.

And why was he remembering that now? He moved so that Savannah was no longer in his eyeline in the mirror. Was it because for the first time since his rugby career had been ended he wished he could be unblemished inside and out? Was it because Savannah Ross was too innocent to know the ugliness inside him?

Realising he was only paying attention to half the things his driver was telling him, he made some token comment and started watching Savannah again. She looked so small and vulnerable, sitting all alone on a sea of cream leather. The Bentley was the right scale for a man his size, but she was dwarfed by it. And she was a distraction he couldn't afford, he warned himself, especially if he was going to remain aloof from her when they reached their destination.

Stately cypress groves provided a lush green counterpoint to the rolling fields of Tuscany, and with the sun burning low in a cobalt sky Savannah wondered if there might be enough beauty here to distract her from her main obsession—but her main obsession turned at that moment to speak to her.

'We'll be arriving at the *palazzo* at the perfect time.'

'Sunset,' Savannah guessed. A thrill of excitement overtook her fear that Ethan had not forgotten or forgiven her for the earlier misunderstanding. As the light faded his face was in shadow, so she couldn't see his expression to gauge his mood, but there was something here that had lifted it—his *palazzo*, she suspected. Following the direction in which he was looking she searched hungrily for her first sight of the building. The sky was a vibrant palette of tangerine and violet so dramatic, so stunningly beautiful, she had butterflies in her stomach at the thought of what might come next. She could sense Ethan was also buzzing with expectation, and try as he might to be stern all the time, an attractive crease had appeared in his face. He'd softened just a little. Now if he could only soften a little more and smile at her that would be a gift—the only gift she wanted.

'When we cross the river, you'll see the *palazzo* in this direction.'

As Ethan pointed towards the shadowy purple hills, she sat bolt upright, tense with expectation.

'I don't want you to miss the approach,' he said, seeing her interest. 'It's quite spectacular.'

'I won't,' she assured him as anticipation fluttered in her stomach. Something told her that this was one of those precious moments that would mean something all her life and must be cherished.

She was only half right, Savannah discovered. When it came into view the *palazzo* exceeded her expectations so far it took her breath away. Rising like something out of a legend from the mist was a winding road and an old stone bridge, and then the towering walls. A glittering snake of water travelled beneath the bridge, and as they crossed it she thought the restless eddies were like mirrored scales carrying the sun-fire to the sea.

'Now you understand why the palazzo got its name.'

Even Ethan couldn't quite keep the excitement from his voice.

'Understatement,' she breathed. The turreted spread of the Palazzo dei Tramonti Dorati appeared framed in fire, and even her fertile imagination hadn't come close to doing it justice. This wasn't the Gothic horror she'd feared Ethan might inhabit, but a palace of light, built from pink stone that might have been sugar-rock. Glowing warm beneath the red-streaked sky, it couldn't have appeared more welcoming.

'What do you think?' Ethan prompted.

Savannah was surprised her opinion mattered to him, and the thought touched her immensely—though she mustn't read too much into it, she reminded herself. 'I think it's stunning,' she told him honestly. 'The colour of the stone is extraordinary.'

'Pink?'

The touch of irony in his voice made her smile. Were they connecting at last? Just a little, maybe? But she wasn't going to push it. 'You must admit, it's unusual,' she said, trying to sound grown up about it, though the prospect of staying in a pink palace, and one as beautiful as this, would have excited anyone.

'The stone is pink because millions of years ago this whole valley was a deep marine-gulf,' Ethan explained. 'The pink hue is due to the millions of tiny shells and fossils locked in the rocks.'

'What a magical explanation.' And romantic, Savannah mused as Ethan settled back to enjoy the last leg of the journey. He might fight as hard as he could to keep his distance from her, but he had brought her to one of the most romantic places on earth. Ethan might shun everything pink or soft or feminine, but he'd let his guard down by showing her his *palazzo*. 'The Palace of the Golden Sunset,' she murmured happily as the limousine made a smooth transition from slick tarmac to the winding cobbled streets.

'Can you see the fragments of the original walls?' Ethan said, turning towards her again.

His enthusiasm was framed in a scholarly tone, but he was clearly determined to share this with her, and he didn't need to tell her how much he loved his *palazzo* when she could feel his passion like a warm cloak embracing her. 'Yes, I see them,' she said, pressing her face to the window. In some places there was little more than raised ground to show where the original walls must have stood, but at others she could see what remained of them.

They looked like blackened silhouettes pointing crooked fingers towards the blazing sky.

'Much of the structure dates from medieval times,' Ethan continued.

Like the thinking of its master? Savannah wondered. What would it take to have Ethan see her as a grown woman rather than as a singing sensation recently signed to his record label? And was she sure she wanted him to think about her that way? Wasn't it safer to remain as she was—a ward under his protection?

It was beyond the scope of Savannah's imagination to conjure up the consequences of attracting the sexual attentions of a man like Ethan, and as the limousine slowed to pass beneath a narrow stone archway she told herself how lucky it was that this was only destined to be a short stay. Any longer and she'd definitely fall in love with him.

The paparazzi would soon find another story and she'd be able to return home. But if she was so confident about that, why was she wracked by shivers of anticipation at the prospect of staying with Ethan?

Because she was tired, Savannah told herself firmly. Who could blame her for feeling uncomfortable with what lay ahead when she was pinned into a dress that felt more like a medieval torture-device than a couture gown?

'This gateway is called the Porta Monteguzzo.'

She paid attention as Ethan distracted her, and was about to answer him when, embarrassingly, her stomach growled.

'Hungry?' he prompted.

'I'm starving,' Savannah admitted, wondering when she had last eaten. And did she dare to eat when another crumb of food on her hips meant she would definitely pop out of Madame's gown and she had no clothes of her own to wear yet? 'Porta Monteguzzo,' she repeated, both in an attempt to distract herself from hunger pangs and to try again to master the musical Italian language. 'Doesn't "*guzzo*" mean "food", in Italian?'

'You're thinking of gusto, perhaps?'

She watched his mouth, thinking how well he spoke the language…amongst other things.

'Which means taste,' Ethan explained.

Or tasty, perhaps, Savannah mused as she turned to stare innocently out of the window while Ethan resumed his conversation in fluent Italian with their driver. But as they drove deeper into Ethan territory and the world he dominated, and those tall, stone walls of his stole the light, Savannah knew that, though the sight of Ethan's fairy-tale castle had thrilled her beyond belief, it had singularly failed to reassure her.

Oh.

Savannah's heart sank as she stood in the hallway of the *palazzo*. It was a struggle to marry up the exquisite exterior with this dismal space. Wasn't it wired for electricity? She could hardly make out the faces of Ethan's staff as he showed her round.

Okay, so maybe that was a slight exaggeration, but the inside of the palace was like something out of a gothic horror film—'dark and dismal' didn't even begin to cover it. It might just as well have been lit by candlelight, it was so shadowy and grim. To say she was disappointed after the stunning run-up to the building was a major understatement. But she was more concerned about the fact that Ethan chose to live like this.

As the housekeeper led the way up the marble staircase, Savannah's apprehension grew. Apart from the very real risk of missing her footing on the dimly lit staircase, the landing they were heading for appeared equally dingy. To go from fairy-tale *palazzo* to the haunted house was a huge disappointment. She only had to contrast Ethan's grand *palazzo* with her parents' simple farmhouse to know there was no contest: she'd prefer the sunny chaos of the farmhouse to this grand grimness any day.

Perhaps she should offer a few home-improvement tips, Savannah concluded as the housekeeper indicated they should follow her down a darkened corridor. 'Don't you worry about your staff tripping over the rugs?' She took the chance to whisper discreetly to Ethan.

'I can't say it's ever occurred to me,' he said with surprise.

'It would occur to me,' Savannah said worriedly as the housekeeper stopped outside a carved-oak door. 'What if someone was carrying a tray with hot drinks on it, or some glasses, and they tripped? They could really hurt themselves, Ethan. This is dangerous. There's hardly any light here at all.'

'No one's ever complained before.'

She knew she should hold her tongue, but it was about time someone did complain, Savannah thought, and Ethan's staff was hardly likely to.

The more she thought about it, the more Savannah became convinced that she must be one of Ethan's first guests at the *palazzo* in a long time. She wasn't sure exactly what she'd been expecting from a man known to be reclusive, but this was hardly the big, open house her family would have filled with light and laughter. She smiled as she thought of the cosy farmhouse back home with its rickety furniture and frayed old rugs, but it was a hundred times more welcoming than this.

The housekeeper was smiling at her expectantly, Savannah realised, quickly refocusing and smiling back.

Ethan was shifting restlessly, as if he couldn't understand the delay before the housekeeper got round to opening a door. But Savannah understood perfectly when the housekeeper finally revealed her surprise.

'*Signorina*, this is your room.'

Savannah didn't need to see the older woman's beaming smile to know that someone was keen to make her feel welcome. 'My room?' Savannah stood on the threshold, gazing in wonder. 'You did this for me?' The contrast between this well-lit space and the rest of the *palazzo* was incredible. No wonder the housekeeper had revealed her surprise with such a flourish.

'You're too generous.' But as Savannah looked at Ethan she realised he was as surprised as she was. He'd had nothing to do with it. His staff had done all this for her. They must have thrown open every window to air the room, and they had certainly lit every available light. There was a log fire blazing in the hearth, which illuminated all the beautiful old oil-paintings, and there were fresh flowers everywhere, beaming a rainbow welcome at her. 'Thank you; thank you so much!' she exclaimed, turning to grasp the housekeeper's hands.

'You bring us music, *signorina*, but all we can bring you in return is flowers.'

'What do you mean "all"?' Savannah exclaimed. 'This means everything to me.'

Tears stung her eyes as she remembered this was the sort of thing her family did for each other at home. The housekeeper had given her the one thing money couldn't buy, and that was a genuine welcome. Conscious of Ethan standing at her side, and knowing how difficult he found dealing with displays of emotion, she expressed her feelings more calmly to him. 'This is wonderful, isn't it?

You have great people working for you. I hope you appreciate them.'

He would think her presumptuous, Savannah realised, though she could read nothing on Ethan's face. But she had to say something, because his staff had carved an oasis of light and beauty for her from his cold, dark *palazzo*, and now she was eager to do the same for him.

He was shocked by his staff's initiative. All he'd done was call ahead to explain the situation to them and ask them to make a room ready for Savannah Ross. He should have known the Italians' great love of music meant they would already know everything about Savannah, and that it would have put wings on their heels when they learned he was bringing her to stay.

As his gaze embraced the room before him, he began noticing things he hadn't before, like the pink-veined, marble-topped console table where the telephone rested. He had bought it with the *palazzo*, and it was a beautiful example of a craftsman's art. Savannah was right; with the light shining on it, the furniture, like everything else in the room, was fully revealed in all its glory. No wonder she had been so relieved to see the efforts his staff had gone to for her. But the real difference here was Savannah, he thought, watching her shimmering golden hair bounce around her shoulders as she followed the housekeeper around the room. Savannah brought the light with her.

With emotions roused that he had thought were long buried, Ethan was suddenly keen to put some distance between them, so he found an excuse to leave Savannah in the care of his housekeeper. But she stubbornly refused to let him disappear so easily. 'I'm so excited,' she told him. 'I can't thank you enough for allowing me to stay here.'

'Then don't. This is nothing to do with me.' He dismissed the glowing room with a gesture.

'You're so wrong,' she assured him. 'This has everything to do with you.'

He shrugged. 'In this instance, Savannah, it is you who is wrong. This is a beautiful suite of rooms and nothing more. It has been aired and put back into use, and that is all.'

'And is that all you have to say about it?' she demanded, frowning.

'What else is there to say? I rarely come here, but it is beautiful, and I had forgotten.'

'But you never will forget again,' she insisted passionately. 'Not now the lights have been switched on.'

He gave her a look that stopped her in her tracks. It was a look intended to warn her not to go this far again. The contact between them was electric, and he let the moment hang for some reason. Anything might have happened as Savannah looked up at him had not his housekeeper coughed discreetly at that moment. It was only then that the rational side of him clicked into focus, and he took a proper look at Savannah and realised how exhausted she looked. She was still wearing his old shirt over the ill-fitting gown. She must have felt embarrassed, dressed that way when he'd introduced her to his staff, but not for a moment had she let it show. Her attention had been all on them, her only thought to make them feel special. 'Could you bring Ms Ross a robe, please?' he asked his housekeeper.

He wanted Savannah covered up. Her pale skin beneath the neck of his shirt was making him restless. She still had her precious sandals dangling from her wrist, like a child with a garish bangle, and she was scarcely taller than a child. She couldn't have eaten since that morning, he remembered. 'Take a bath,' he said briskly, 'And then use that phone over there to call down for something to eat.'

'Won't you eat something too?' she asked with concern.

'Maybe.' He dismissed her with a gesture. He had no intention of prolonging this encounter. It occurred to him then that perhaps he didn't trust himself to prolong it.

'Where will you eat?' she pressed as he prepared to leave.

He hadn't given it a moment's thought. 'I'll take dinner in my room,' he said, remembering that that was what he usually did.

'In your room?' She pulled a face, and then immediately grew contrite. 'Sorry. It's none of my business where you eat.'

No, it isn't, he almost informed her, thinking of her other comments since they'd arrived, but the fact that she looked so pale held him back.

Fortunately his housekeeper returned at that moment with the robe, which put a halt to further conversation.

He took that as his cue. 'Goodnight, Savannah. Sleep well.'

'I'll see you in the morning?' Her eyes were wide, her expression frank.

'Perhaps.' With her innocent enthusiasm she made it hard for him to remain distant.

'For breakfast?' she pressed.

'Ah…' He paused with his hand on the door, as if to say he was a much older man with many better things to do than to entertain a young woman. 'We'll see.'

'Sleep well, Ethan. And thank you once again for allowing me to stay in your beautiful home.'

Who should be thanking who? he wondered, catching

sight of the luminous expression on his housekeeper's face. 'Goodnight, Savannah.' He didn't need a second dose of Savannah's radiant face before he walked out and closed the door to know his defences had been breached.

CHAPTER SEVEN

SAVANNAH waited for Ethan's footsteps to fade before asking the housekeeper shyly, 'Do you think it would be possible to put on some more lights?' The housekeeper had been so kind to her that Savannah felt her request might have some chance of success.

'More lights, *signorina*?'

'In the *palazzo*? I mean, it's very dark outside my room, and I just thought it might be safer for you—for all of us.'

The housekeeper studied Savannah's face before deciding. 'Come with me, *signorina*.'

As they left the room together the housekeeper called to a passing footman, who looked at Savannah with surprise when he heard her request via the housekeeper. As he hurried away, the housekeeper exchanged a look with Savannah. 'You are starting a revolution,' she confided.

'Oh dear.'

'No, it's good.'

'Is it?' If only she could feel confident that Ethan would agree.

Savannah approached the first light-switch.

It took all of her resolve just to switch it on. But when she did…

'*Bellissima!*' The housekeeper exclaimed, clasping her hands in front of her. 'This is what the *palazzo* has been waiting for.'

Her endorsement encouraged Savannah to ask if they could put a few more lights on.

The housekeeper drew in a breath and then, exhaling slowly, she turned to look at Savannah. Her eyes were sparkling. 'A very few,' she agreed. 'Let's do it!'

They hurried off in different directions, snapping on light switches like naughty children, and they didn't stop until the whole of the upper floor was flooded with light.

Down in the hallway Savannah could see more lights being turned on. It was like the curtain going up at the theatre, she concluded, feeling that same sense of wonder—but the only difference here was a glorious home was being revealed rather than a stage set.

The housekeeper rendezvoused with Savannah back at her room. 'It's amazing!' Savannah exclaimed softly, gazing at the transformation they'd created.

'*Si, signorina.* You have worked a miracle.'

'A very tiny miracle,' Savannah argued with a smile. 'I only turned on the lights.'

'Sometimes that's all it takes,' the older woman observed shrewdly.

They shared a smile before the housekeeper left Savannah, after asking her to promise she would call downstairs if she needed anything more.

Well, she would need all the friends she could find on the staff, if she stood a chance of leaving Ethan's home happier than she had found it, Savannah reflected. But with all his beautiful treasures bathed in light she had to believe he would share her enthusiasm for ancient frescoes stepping out of the shadows, and carvings revealed in all their intricate detail after years of neglect.

But…would he be pleased, or would he be angry at her continued interference? She was only a guest, after all, and one that wasn't here for very long. She suspected she knew why Ethan avoided light, but her concern was for the main thoroughfares where safety was an issue. The more intimate areas like Ethan's rooms could remain discreetly lit. She could only hope he would agree it was a happy balance.

Deep inside, Savannah believed everyone needed light. And as for the *palazzo*, well, she'd already seen the results of the transformation Ethan's staff had brought about in her rooms, and their instincts were right. There should be light, love and music in such a beautiful home. There should be life at the *palazzo*.

Savannah took a long, soapy bath. Now the excitement was over, she realised how hungry she was, and until supper arrived a bath was the perfect distraction from hunger pangs as well as from the likely repercussions of her interference in Ethan's home.

Twiddling the taps with her toes, she sank a little lower in the fragrant bubbles. This story might not have a happy-ever-after ending, but she had fairy-tale accommodation for the night, and after the staff had gone to so much trouble it would have been churlish for her to refuse the setting they had prepared.

She had rifled through the full-sized luxury products on the glass shelves like a small child in a beauty salon, and now the scent rising from the steam had led her into a dream world of erotic images in which Ethan starred…

Wrapped up cosily in a warm robe some time later, she

stared into the mirror. It was so easy to imagine Ethan's dark face when she saw him in the shadows everywhere she went. It was torture, knowing he was somewhere close by, and almost impossible not to imagine him stripped and naked beneath an ice-cold shower. It would be cold water, because warm was too indulgent for him. And his bedroom would be spartan, she decided, because Ethan denied himself anything soft or superfluous— which didn't leave her with too much hope, Savannah concluded wistfully.

Rubbing her hair vigorously, she walked back into the bedroom. Kneeling in front of the fire to dry her long hair, she thought about Ethan's complex character. All he seemed to need was a clean bed and a floor to pace— perhaps with the addition of a giant television-screen in every room to catch up on any rugby matches he might have missed. Perhaps it was the legacy of those dreadful scars that made him so careless of his own comfort.

Thinking about them always made her so angry. Casting the towel aside, she began to pluck distractedly at the rug. Who would do that to him? Who could do that to a fellow human being?

Why don't you ask him? Savannah's inner voice prompted.

Because life isn't that simple?

But it could be, if she went to him, and spoke to him…

Rolling onto her back, Savannah stared up at the ornate plasterwork. All the *palazzo* could be like this, cared for and fully restored, and always welcoming. Or it could remain cold and full of shadows. How lonely it must be to live in the dark.

Sitting bolt upright, Savannah hugged her knees and, resting her chin, she stared into the fire. It didn't have to be like this if someone changed it around—if she changed it around. An impossible task, perhaps, but not if she had the help of Ethan's staff. Even this gleaming fireguard, polished to a flawless sheen, was evidence of their care for him. They had to be as keen as she was to see the *palazzo* come back to life.

Impatient with inaction, she sprang up. She hardly knew where she was going, but as she crossed the room her spirits lifted. It was such a glorious ultra-feminine space it must have given Ethan a headache just to poke his head round the door. Everything that wasn't gilded or twinkling glass was covered in silk, satins or velvet, and all in the most exquisite pastel colours. Stretching out her arms, she turned full circle, thinking it the most appealing space she had ever inhabited. She was still smiling broadly when she reached the door and opened it. 'Ethan!'

'Savannah.'

She knew immediately from his voice that Ethan was furious. She felt instantly guilty, as well as silly and awkward, standing barefoot in front of him in her towelling robe. Her lips trembled and her smile died instantly.

'What have you done?' he snapped.

Her gaze slid away. 'I was taking a bath.'

'You know I don't mean that.'

Savannah drew her robe a little closer, conscious that Ethan's stare was boring into her, demanding an answer.

'I mean the lights,' he explained. 'I take it you're responsible?'

'Yes, I switched them on. Please don't be angry with your staff, Ethan.' She touched his arm. 'It was all my fault. I did it for them, for you.'

'For me? For them? What is this nonsense?'

Tears were threatening. She had been so looking

forward to sharing this moment with him, Savannah realised, and now it had all gone wrong. Far from wanting light, Ethan craved the darkness to hide his scars. She should have known and not been so insensitive. In trying to help him she had arrogantly assumed she was right, only seeing the world from her own perspective. And now he couldn't wait to turn those lights off, or for her to leave. 'I'm so sorry—'

'You'll have to leave,' he said, perfectly echoing her thoughts. 'I can't have this sort of interference. Please pack your bags.'

'Ethan—'

'There's nothing more to say, Savannah.'

'But it's nighttime. Where will I go?'

'A hotel, the airport, somewhere—I don't care.'

'You're throwing me out?'

'Save your melodrama for the stage.'

'Says you, living in the dark!' She couldn't believe she'd said that. But it was true. She was fighting for Ethan, and where that was concerned nothing she said was going too far. But as Ethan's stony stare raked her face, Savannah realised he didn't see it that way.

'Will you pack?' he said coldly, confirming her worst fears. 'Or must I call the housekeeper to do that for you?'

'Ethan, please.' It was no use. He'd closed off to her.

As he shook Savannah's hand from his arm, he saw her tears and his heart ignored the dictates of his head.

'Please don't be angry with your housekeeper,' she entreated, adding to the conflict boiling inside him. 'You must know this is all my fault.'

Every bit of it was Savannah's fault...or her blessing. He turned his back so he wouldn't have to look into her face, but still he felt her goodness washing over him. She wouldn't stop until all the bitterness was cleaned away. She touched his arm, begging him. 'You've gone too far,' he growled, wanting even now to protect her from that black evil inside him.

She didn't argue, and instead she did something far worse: she confessed.

'You're right,' she said frankly. 'I interfered where I shouldn't have. This is your home, Ethan, not mine. I asked your staff to turn on some lights so it was safer for them, and for you. I can see I went too far with that plan when one or two lights would have been sufficient, and if you want me to leave I will. All I ask is your promise that you won't blame your staff for my thoughtless actions.'

He didn't need to see any more tears to know that Savannah was at her most vulnerable. Yet she fought on in the defence of others. He couldn't ignore that. Her appeal had touched him deeply in a way he hadn't felt, maybe, ever. He was still wondering how best to deal with this unusual situation when the housekeeper Savannah was at such pains to defend came unwittingly to their rescue.

'Something to eat, *signore, signorina*?' she said blithely when Savannah opened the door to her knock.

What perfect timing, Savannah thought, exhaling with relief as she smiled at her new friend. As her shoulders relaxed she quickly adapted her manner so as not to concern the older woman. 'Let me take that tray from you.'

'No, please, let me.' Ethan's innate good manners meant he had to step forward in front of Savannah to take the tray himself.

'Thank you, *signore*,' the housekeeper said politely, handing Ethan the tray without any sign that she had over-heard their heated exchange. 'I've made enough for two.'

Hmm, Savannah thought, realising Ethan had no other option other than to carry the tray into her room. 'Let me clear a space for you,' she said, hurrying ahead of him.

To give her a moment to regroup, she rushed about, hunting for her slippers. Ethan placed the tray down on the low table between the two sofas and remained standing.

This was one consequence she could not avoid.

By the time she had found her slippers and slipped them on, she could hardly breathe, let alone speak as she came to a halt in front of Ethan.

When exactly had he become so hard and unfeeling? She had only turned the lights on, after all, which in the bright world Savannah inhabited was a very small transgression. As she ran her fingers through her still-damp hair, her face naked after her shower, he knew she was also naked under her robe. She looked nervous, apprehensive; fearful. She was certainly braced for a stinging rebuke. 'We shouldn't let the supper go to waste. That's if you don't mind…'

She looked surprised at his suggestion, as he had expected, but she quickly rallied, saying, 'Of course I don't mind. Please, sit down. You must be hungry too?'

'A little,' he admitted.

Savannah had to stop audibly sighing with relief as Ethan sat down. Maybe there was a chance, however slender, that she could change things for him before she left; it was all she wanted. But as always in the world of Savannah things never ran according to plan. She remembered that her underwear for the next day, having been rinsed out, was still hanging over the bath—large, comfy knickers included. What if he decided to go in there? 'D'you mind, if I…?' Flapping her hands, she glanced anxiously across the room.

'Not at all. Take your time,' Ethan invited.

She would have to, Savannah thought, resting back against the bathroom door. She wasn't leaving this room until her heartbeat steadied, which meant she could be in here quite some time. Ethan was full of surprises. She felt like he was giving her a second chance. But he was so complex, she had no idea what to expect next. But then she hardly knew him, Savannah reasoned. When she emerged from the bathroom, there was music playing.

'Do you like it?' Ethan asked as Savannah poked her head self-consciously round the door.

'Is it what I think it is?'

'If you think it's your first CD then, yes, it is.'

Savannah pulled back inside the bathroom, suffused with too many emotions to impose them on Ethan. She felt elated that her teachers' and parents' dreams for her had come true, and dread that Ethan only regarded her as a property belonging to his record label.

'Aren't you coming out to join me?' he called. 'Come and listen to your music.'

She could hardly refuse, since Ethan owned the record company. 'Do you like it?' she said anxiously when she returned.

'Like it? Your singing voice always makes me think of…'

Frogs croaking? Wheels grinding?

'Birds singing,' he said, settling back with a blissful expression on his face as Savannah's voice filled the room. 'Song birds,' he added dryly, without opening his eyes.

At least not crows squawking.

She should have more confidence, Savannah told herself, but in many ways she was as happy in the shadows as Ethan. In a different way, of course. But she loved nothing more than the wide-open countryside back home, and the fact that she could walk for miles unnoticed as she soaked up all the glories of nature.

'I'm glad we signed you.'

Savannah refocused to find Ethan staring thoughtfully at her. 'Thank you.' She risked a small smile as her heart drummed wildly.

'You should eat something. It must be hours since you last ate.'

Probably. She had no idea. But she would have to lean past him to take something, and she was acutely aware that she was naked under her robe.

'Here,' he said, offering her the loaded plate. 'Take one of these delicious *ciabatta*.'

'Ethan, if I've offended you—'

'Eat something, Savannah, before you faint.'

'I didn't mean to,' she finished softly. 'Sometimes my enthusiasm carries me away.'

He hummed at this and angled his stubble-shaded chin towards the plate.

'Thank you.' Selecting a delicious-looking, well-filled roll, she bit into it with relish, expressing her pleasure in a series of appreciative sounds. Even now, beneath Ethan's unforgiving eye, she couldn't hide her feelings. 'You're very lucky to have such wonderful staff.'

'Yes, I am.' And when she thought that short statement was it, he added, 'You were right about the gloom making life difficult for them. And, yes, even dangerous. And, as for artworks, I hadn't even noticed.' He paused and then admitted, 'Who would think turning on the lights could make such a difference?'

She could.

CHAPTER EIGHT

ETHAN realised how much he had misjudged Susannah when his housekeeper, having returned with a fresh plate of food, took him to one side to inform him that she was glad to see how happy the *piccola signorina* was now the lights were on.

The way the older woman had held his gaze suggested more than the fact that Savannah was a guest with particular tastes to accommodate, or even that his housekeeper liked the young singer and wanted to make her stay as comfortable as possible. It was more the type of look the older generation gave the younger in Italy—and would sometimes be accompanied by tapping the side of the nose. Naturally, the older woman wouldn't dream of being so familiar with him, but she had got her message across. He'd brushed off her inquisitiveness with a rare smile.

Some time ago he had come to understand and even envy the Italian nation's fixation with love. And how could he be angry with Savannah, when all it took to make him smile was to watch her sucking her fingers with gusto before devouring another sandwich? Savannah had transformed the *palazzo* in the short time she'd been here, filling it with good things and raising the spirits of his staff. It wouldn't last when she'd gone, of course, but she had unlocked one small portion of his heart, which was good news for his staff.

'It is a beautiful room, isn't it?'

As Savannah lifted her head with surprise, he realised he was seeing things through her eyes and how different things could be if he decided to make them so.

She'd go mad with grief if she heard that Ethan had returned to his old ways when she went home. And that wasn't overreaction, it was pure, hard fact, Savannah concluded, blushing when, having held the door for his housekeeper, Ethan remained leaning against the door frame with his powerful arms folded across his chest, watching her.

Her body reacted as if Ethan had just made the most indecent suggestion. His tight fitting T-shirt strained hard across his chest, and his jeans were secured with a heavy-duty belt. She had noticed all this in the space of a few seconds, and started nervously when Ethan moved.

'More sandwiches?' he suggested, strolling across the room towards her.

She was as tense as a doe at bay, Savannah realised, sitting straight. 'No, thank you.'

And then she decided she had better get up and clear some space on the table for all the new food, but being nervous and clumsy she moved erratically, and somehow a chair leg got in her way. Ethan called out, but it was too late, and as he reached out to grab her to stop her falling she ended up in his arms.

'Suddenly you've got more legs than a millipede, and each one of them travelling in a different direction,' he suggested.

'Pretty much,' she admitted, though the millipede analogy failed to grow on her. A better woman would have made the most of this opportunity, while all she could think was had she cleaned her teeth?

'Well, I'm still hungry,' he admitted, letting her go and heading back to the sofa.

She watched him stretch out his muscular legs, knowing she had never felt more awkward in her life. And yes—thank the dentist's warnings—she had cleaned her teeth, but Savannah Ross was about to play host to Ethan Alexander? It hardly seemed possible.

'Won't you help me?' He glanced her way as he reached for a sandwich. 'My housekeeper clearly thinks we both need feeding up.'

Or perhaps the older woman wanted to keep him here, Savannah thought, surprising herself with this reflection. They ate in silence until Savannah put down her napkin with a sigh of contentment. The hearty feed had reminded her of home.

'You were hungry,' Ethan commented, wiping his lips on a napkin.

As he continued to stare at her, Savannah's cheeks heated up. They were still talking about food, weren't they?

Of course they were, she reasoned, smoothing out her hair, or rather the tangles. What must Ethan think of her, bare faced and barely dressed? Having never entertained a man before whilst naked beneath a robe, she wasn't too sure of the protocol. And as Ethan still showed no sign of going anywhere, she suggested, 'Why don't I switch on the television?' Maybe they'd catch the news, she reasoned.

'The television?'

'I just thought maybe there would be a news report about the match...or us.' Her cheeks fired up as Ethan gave her a look. The word 'us' couldn't have carried more embarrassing weight had it tried.

'I try to escape the news when I'm here.' Ethan's tone was a chilling return to his former manner.

'But surely not items affecting your business—or world affairs—or sport?' She was running out of options, wishing she knew how to turn the clock back so she could remove all reference to 'us'.

'No,' he said bluntly. 'And, Savannah, I need to tell you something.'

By which time she'd switched on the set. Her timing was impeccable, Savannah realised, recoiling as she blenched. 'Why, that's ridiculous!' A news item had just flashed up on the screen. A news item featuring Ethan Alexander caught out, so the reporters said, with his latest squeeze, a young ingénue only recently signed to his record label.

'How could such a nice evening end so badly?' Ethan wondered, glancing at her.

Now she knew why he hadn't wanted her to turn it on. 'How can you take it so well?'

'Because I know what to expect. That's one of the reasons I came to find you. I wanted to tell you myself before you found out by some other means. But now...' Leaning across her, picking up the remote-control and pointing it at the set, he switched it off.

'Shouldn't we know everything before we do that?' Savannah exclaimed. Terrible lies were being told about them. 'Don't you care what they're saying about us?'

'Do I care about gossip?'

'Gossip? They're telling lies!'

Ethan responded calmly. 'What are they going to do? They'll soon tire of us, and in no time those pictures will be wrapped around somebody's fish and chips.'

'A famous tycoon saves the girl with the golden tonsils, blushes, in front of a worldwide television audience?' Savannah stuck a finger in her mouth to show what she thought of that. 'A story like that could run and run.'

'Gossip only hurts you if you allow it to,' Ethan told her evenly. 'And if you're going to let it get you down like this, Savannah, perhaps you should have another think about pursuing a career in the public eye.'

Were those her marching orders? She went cold immediately, thinking of all the people who had helped her along the way and who would be badly let down if she quit. 'But the press say we're sleeping together.' Surely that would get through to him?

Ethan's brow rose seductively. 'Is that so bad?'

He shouldn't tease her. Savannah's cheeks flushed crimson the moment he put the thought of them being sexually involved into her head. And why was he doing that when he had vowed not to think of Savannah as anything other than a young girl under his protection? Was it because sometimes a deeper feeling than common sense took the lead?

Before he had a chance to reason it through she begged him to switch on the set again so she could know the worst. She made him smile inwardly. Her voice was shaking with anger, not fear, and her hands were balled into fists as if she would like to punch out the screen. She was new to this, he remembered. 'You know what they're saying and so do I,' he soothed, 'So let them get on with it.'

'No,' she shot back fiercely. 'We have to issue a denial.'

'We have something to deny?' he queried, pouncing on her naivety before it had a chance to take root. Picking up the remote-control which she had cunningly re-claimed, he tossed it out of her reach.

Gradually she relaxed, hopefully seeing the sense behind his years of doing battle with the press. 'Thank goodness my parents are away,' she said, confirming this.

She looked so grateful it drove home the message that Savannah came from a strong and loving family. He couldn't shake a lingering sense of loss for something he'd never had. But her desire to go out and slay dragons soon distracted him. The expression on her face was so appealing.

It took Savannah a moment to realise Ethan was laughing. It was the first time she'd heard him laugh, without it being an ugly or mocking sound. 'What's so funny?'

He shook his head, unable to speak for a moment. 'The infamous hard man and his teenage songbird?' he managed at last. 'They make us sound like something out of a novel.'

'And I'm not a teenager,' Savannah pointed out. 'I was twenty last week.'

'Twenty?' Ethan's face stilled. 'As old as that?'

'Well, I'm not some teenage tweety-pie, if that's what you think—and I think we should sue them,' she said seriously, which only made him start laughing again.

'You can if you like,' Ethan suggested between bouts of laughter.

Using magic beans to pay the lawyers, presumably. But as she had a leading role in this mess she was deter-mined to do something about it.

'From my point of view.'

'Yes?' Savannah stared intently at Ethan, ready to jump

into armour and fight at his side at the first sign he was preparing to take on the press.

'I think you should ignore it, as I will. Unless—' he held up his hands when she was about to leap in '—they become a nuisance, in which case I shall act.'

That was just so disappointing. She didn't want to sit back and have rubbish thrown at her. She was about to challenge Ethan's decision when a knock came at the door and her bags from the stadium arrived.

'I haven't let you down yet, have I?' Ethan demanded as she checked them over. 'And I'm not about to start now. And where this newspaper rubbish is concerned you'll just have to try something new.'

'Such as?' Lifting her head, she stared at him.

'You could try trusting me.'

'But we're trapped here,' she pointed out.

'Yes, in this terrible place,' Ethan mocked gently. 'Poor us.'

He only had to say this for warning darts of fire to attack every part of her, and each tiny arrow carried a subtle message. She wanted him, but confronted by Ethan's worldliness, and by the thought of staying under his roof, she grabbed the edges of her robe and tugged it firmly shut. 'Haven't they've got anything better to do than speculate about us?'

'They're only doing their job,' Ethan pointed out. 'We're newsworthy. You. Me. Both of us together. Now that's a real story.'

'But this isn't a real story. They've twisted the truth and made innocent photographs seem so…'

'Suggestive?'

She hadn't wanted to say that, and when Ethan looked at her a certain way she wished she hadn't. Prior to this she had been sure Ethan thought of her as a ward beneath his protection, and the thought that he was now looking at her as a woman was unsettling. It might be everything she had ever dreamed of, but as fantasy hurtled towards reality at breakneck pace she lost her nerve. Getting up, she assured him, 'Well, don't worry, if I do have to stay here for any length of time, I'll keep right out of your way.'

'How very thoughtful of you,' Ethan murmured. 'Tea?' he proposed. 'Hot and sweet, perhaps?' he added under his breath. 'It's good for shock.' He reached for the phone to call the kitchen.

Shock? He thought she was in shock? She probably *was* in shock after seeing the news bulletin, Savannah conceded. But tea? She didn't want tea. 'I think I need something stronger than that.'

Ethan held the phone away from his ear. 'Espresso?'

His face was poker straight, but his eyes were laughing at her. This humorous side of him—so unsuspected, so attractive—was unbelievably seductive. And terrifying. She had no idea how to handle a man—any man—let alone a man like Ethan. The situation was rapidly spiralling out of control. 'Gin and tonic, please,' she said firmly, thinking it might help. 'A large one.'

For a moment she thought Ethan might refuse, but then he crossed the room to the wet bar where he mixed a drink. At last he was treating her like someone over the age of consent.

'Here you are,' he said pleasantly, handing her the glass. 'I hope I got the balance right?'

She took a large swig in a pathetic attempt to maintain a confident image—and choked. Worse than choked she wheezed and choked, whilst waving her hands frantically in the air as fire consumed her gullet.

'So, you're a virgin,' he said with amusement.

She was aghast that he could tell. 'How did you know?'

Holding the crystal tumbler aloft, he stared into the clear liquid. 'You can't drink a decent measure of alcohol without…' His voice tailed away as he looked at her. 'Oh, I see. We're not talking about the same thing, are we? Well, are we, Savannah?' Ethan pressed, and, far from being humorous now, his expression was grim.

She couldn't answer. Her throat had seized up with embarrassment. In the silence that followed everything Ethan had ever thought about her seemed to grow in her mind to grotesque proportions. She was too young for him, too inexperienced, too naïve, and whatever hopes she'd ever had about them ever being together had just turned into dust. But that didn't stop her wanting him, it just pushed him further away, because Ethan was so principled he would never even think of making love to her, believing her innocence was under his charge.

A virgin? *A virgin!* Ethan recoiled inwardly. This made the situation so much worse. How much worse he could hardly quantify in thought, let alone words. Savannah was only here to enjoy his protection, yet until a minute ago he had arrogantly contemplated seducing her. She was still so young, and his first thought must always be to protect her. He had to hang onto that thought now if he was to save her from the greatest danger of all, which was him—the very man who was supposed to be taking care of her.

'Ethan, please don't be angry with me,' she begged him as he made for the door.

'Angry with you?' He was bemused she could think that. 'Goodnight, Savannah.'

'Ethan, please.'

He was halfway through the door when she ran towards him. 'Sleep well,' he said, closing the door firmly behind him with Savannah on the other side. He didn't trust himself to wait and listen to her reply.

She sat on the bed for a long time after Ethan left. With her arms pressed tightly on the top of her head, she knew she'd made such a hash of everything and that she didn't have a clue how to make it right. She had known for some time now that she loved Ethan. How could she care for anyone as deeply as she did for him and not love him? But he still frightened her. She had played a foolish game of make-believe. The first time Ethan had noticed she was a woman, she had taken fright, and now his principles meant they could never be together. *Well done, Savannah*, she congratulated herself; there'd be no encores here.

Climbing off the bed, she went to stare into the mirror. What did Ethan see when he stared in his? He lived his life in spite of his injuries. He had triumphed over them. Or had he? Was she only seeing Ethan's public face? Did those scars torment him when he was alone? Because she cared about him, she couldn't stop thinking about it. How could she leave Tuscany and Ethan with so many things unresolved? She would go to him and speak to him. She would reason with him in the hope that when she went away they could at least be friends.

The fact that she didn't have a clue what she was going to say was immaterial, Savannah thought, tugging on her jeans. This was just one of those moments when doing nothing wasn't an option. She refused to have Ethan think she was repulsed by his scars, or that she made a habit of accepting hospitality and then changing everything around for her host. Caring about someone came with responsibility, which meant she couldn't turn her back on him. And as this might be her last chance to search beneath Ethan's public persona, and find the real man underneath, she had no intention of wasting it.

CHAPTER NINE

MAYBE the fates had decided she deserved a bit of luck, Savannah concluded as she followed a group of servants carrying fresh towels and a tray with a pot of coffee on it. There couldn't be that many people staying at the *palazzo*, surely?

All she cared about was finding Ethan, and as she waited, concealed in the shadows while one of the servants knocked on a door, she thrilled at the sound of his voice. Finding him filled her with relief.

She waited for the staff to come out again, and when their footsteps had died away she came out of hiding and cautiously approached the door around which they'd been clustered. The handle yielded all too easily, and as she pressed the door open a crack she could hear the shower running.

Opening the door fully, Savannah slipped inside. She found herself in a mannish-looking sitting room where the scent of good leather and books was overwhelming. She looked around. Okay, so now what? There was hardly anywhere to hide. As she had suspected, Ethan's tastes were plain. The floors were polished wood, and the sofas were dark-brown leather. The walls were lined with books and not much else, other than some vibrant modern paintings.

Originals, Savannah noted with interest, signed with a letter B that had a diagonal line through it. She could imagine what a psychologist might make of that. And as for the content: frightened, wide-eyed children without faces or proper form. The paintings were brilliant—but, in the same way Edvard Munch's *The Scream* both fascinated and repelled, these paintings were deeply disturbing. And there were shadows in them…lots and lots of shadows.

Were the paintings an autobiographical account of Ethan's childhood?

She'd bet her life on it. And this window into his psyche was both more illuminating and far worse than anything she had imagined. That he had immense talent was in no doubt, and as another type of artist she found that bond between them reassuring—though everything else about the paintings troubled her and told her she was right to be concerned. Listening, she was reassured to hear the shower still running. What other secrets could she uncover in the time she had?

She wasn't here to pry, but to sense things, Savannah told herself, remaining motionless in the middle of the room. And then the water stopped running. And she was completely exposed. She braced herself. All the clever words and questions she'd been preparing for Ethan deserted her. But when he didn't emerge from the bathroom curiosity got the better of her. Tip-toeing to the door, she peeped through a crack. Sensation streamed through every inch of her at the sight of Ethan standing in front of a mirror with just a towel around him.

He was magnificent.

Although his scars were far, far worse than she had thought, she had never seen anyone half so virile or appealing. His legs were beautifully shaped and muscular, and his naked torso was everything she had dreamed of. The extent of his injuries, of his scarring, only proved it was a miracle he had made it through, and the thought of the pain he must have experienced cut her like a knife. He was twice the man she'd thought him. And more.

Savannah jumped back in alarm as Ethan thrust his fists down on a marble counter-top. For a moment she thought he'd seen her and that that must have prompted the angry action, but then she realised he was leaning over his braced arms with his shoulder-muscles knotted and his head bowed, as if the sight of his own body had disgusted him. She knew then that everything she had feared for him was true: Ethan's injuries had scarred more than his body, they had scarred the man.

'Savannah?'

She gasped out loud as he wheeled around.

'Savannah! I'm speaking to you!'

The ferocity in his tone made her back away.

'What do you think you're doing here?'

'Looking for you…' She backed away, hands outstretched in supplication. 'I knocked, but you didn't hear me.'

'You didn't hear the water running?'

'I heard it, but.'

'You didn't leave immediately?'

'No, I.'

'You what?' he flashed across her. 'Wanted to try out your amateur psychology on me?' As he spoke his glance swept the paintings which he knew she must have seen. 'I thought so,' he spat out with contempt when she didn't reply.

'Ethan, please.'

'I thought we'd agreed you'd stay away from me?'

'Did we?' Her voice was trembling. 'I don't remember that.'

Straightening up, Ethan dipped his head. His stare was menacing.

'Stop trying to intimidate me.' If only her voice would stop shaking.

'Then tell me why you're here.'

'Like I said, I was looking for you.'

'Because?' he prompted harshly.

'I wanted to speak to you.'

'And so you sneaked into my room?'

'No!'

'Go back to bed, Savannah.'

'No.' She shook her head. But how was she going to put all her thoughts and impressions into a few short sentences when Ethan would never give her the time? Shorthand was her only option. 'I care about you.'

'You care about me?' Ethan's laugh was cold and ugly. 'If you only knew how infantile that sounded.'

'Caring for someone is infantile?' Savannah threw up her hands. 'Then I'm guilty.' The feelings she had developed for Ethan were so deep and so complex, at this point she had nothing to lose. 'I'll admit, I'm not good with words.'

'No, you're not.' Grabbing his robe, Ethan threw it on, belting it to hide his mutilations from her gaze. 'Get out of here, Savannah.'

'I'm not going anywhere,' she informed him stubbornly.

'Must I throw you out?'

She wanted to run as far and as fast as she could from the expression on Ethan's face. He had turned so angry and dark, and so utterly contemptuous of her. 'You wouldn't—'

But her voice wobbled and Ethan pounced. 'Can you be sure of that?'

'I'm absolutely sure you would never hurt me.' Standing her ground, she stared him full in the face.

'Have you finished? Can I continue with my evening in peace now?'

'I've not nearly finished!' Like a cork in a bottle her frustrations had been tamped down long enough. 'You can't dismiss me. I'm not a child!'

'You certainly look like one to me.'

'Then you're not looking closely enough. I'm a woman, Ethan, a woman with feelings; a woman who won't let those feelings go just because you say I must.'

Ethan's answer was to curtly angle his chin towards the door. 'And now I'm asking you to leave.'

'I'm not going anywhere.'

He tried sweet reason. 'It's been a long day and you should be in bed.'

Savannah shook her head. 'I'm not a child you can order to bed. All I want to do is talk to you.'

'Well, I'm right out of conversation. Now, get out of here. Out!' He backed her towards the door. 'Try to get this through your head, Savannah…' Bringing his face so close she could see the amber flecks in his steel-grey eyes, Ethan ground out, 'I don't want your company. I don't want your conversation. And most of all I don't want you snooping around here, spying on me.'

'I'm not spying on you,' Savannah said, raising her voice too. 'And if it's these you're worried about—'

Sucking air between his teeth, Ethan knocked her hand away, but, ignoring him, she reached up anyway. Touching his face with her fingertips, she traced his cruel scars. 'I don't see them.'

'You don't see them?' Ethan mimicked scathingly. Rearing back, he turned his face away.

'No, I don't.' Savannah flinched as Ethan walked past her. And flinched again when, having poured a glass of water and drained it, he slammed the glass down so hard she couldn't believe it hadn't smashed. 'It's no use you trying to shut me out, because I'm not going anywhere, Ethan.'

He remained with his hostile back turned to her. Perhaps she had gone too far this time. Ethan's massive shoulders were hunched, and his fists were planted so aggressively on a chair back his knuckles gleamed white.

'Bad enough you're here,' he growled without looking at her, 'But you should have told me you were—'

'I'm sorry?' Savannah interrupted, reading his mind. 'Do you mean I should have told you I was a virgin?' She waited until Ethan turned to face her. 'Are you seriously suggesting I should have said, "how do you do, my name is Savannah, and I'm a virgin"?'

'No, of course not,' Ethan snapped, eyes smouldering with passion. 'But if you'd given me at least some intimation, I could have made arrangements for you to stay elsewhere.'

'In a nunnery, perhaps?' Savannah cut across him. 'In a safe place with a chaperon?'

'And this isn't safe, and I don't have a chaperon.'

'Correct.'

As they glared at each other it soon became apparent that neither one of them was prepared to break the stand-off.

'And if I tell you I feel quite safe here with you?'

'And if I tell you that the rest of the world will put a very different construction on your staying here with me?'

'But I thought you didn't care about gossip?' she countered.

'I care how it affects you.'

'From the point of view that I'm signed to your record

company as the next *young* singing sensation, which means I must appear to the world to be innocent?'

Ethan took her barbed comment with far better grace than she might have expected. It was almost as if they had got the measure of each other, and for once he was crediting her with some sense—though he drew out the waiting time until her nerves were flayed and tender. Relaxing onto one hip then, he thumbed his chin as the expression in his eyes slowly cooled from passion to wry reflection. 'That's a very cynical attitude for a young girl to have.'

'How many times—?'

'Must you tell me you're not the young girl I think you are?' he supplied in a low voice that strummed her senses.

'If I'm cynical,' Savannah countered, 'Surely you're the last person who should be surprised?'

'I'm going to say this as clearly as I can.' Ethan's voice held a crushing note of finality. 'I don't want you here. Please leave now.'

She waited a moment too, and then said, 'No.'

'No?'

'No,' Savannah repeated. 'You're asking me to believe I must do everything you say. Well, standing my ground where you're concerned might not be a big thing in your world, or easy in mine, but it has to be a whole lot better than agreeing to be your doormat.'

'Have you quite finished?' he demanded.

'I've barely started,' she assured him, but even she could see there was little point in pursuing this if she couldn't persuade Ethan to see her in a different light.

And she couldn't. He pointed to the door.

Lifting her head, she wrapped what little dignity she had left around her and walked towards it—but when she reached it she just had to know: 'What's wrong with me, Ethan?'

'Wrong with you?' He frowned.

'Is it because I'm not pretty enough, not desirable enough, or is it the fact that I'm not experienced and savvy enough when it comes to handling situations like this?'

'Savannah, there is no situation—other than my increasing impatience with you, which means there may soon be a situation, and it will be one you won't like.'

Walking over to the door, Ethan opened it for her. 'Goodnight, Savannah.'

Ethan felt nothing for her and she had no answer to that. She was so lacking in female guile, she had no tricks up her sleeve, and it was too late to wish she'd learned them before she'd come here.

'What do you think you're doing?' Ethan demanded when she turned around and walked back in the room.

If he wanted her out, he was going to have to throw her out, and something told her he wouldn't do that. Now she just had to hope she was right.

He shook his head. 'Savannah, you are the most difficult, the most stubborn—'

'Individual in the world aside from you?' She held Ethan's gaze along with her breath, and sent a plea into the ether. If there was anyone listening out there, anyone at all…

'I was about to say, the most annoying guest I've ever had. You will have noted my use of the past tense, I hope?'

'You can't just dismiss me.'

'Watch me. Out,' he rapped, employing the full force of his laser stare.

'Why are you so angry all the time?'

'Why are you so slow to take a hint?'

'Well, clearly my experience of men is somewhat limited, but if you'd just allow me to—'

'To do what?' he cut across her, eyes narrowed in suspicion.

'Spend time with you?' Savannah trembled as she clutched on to this last all-too-brittle straw.

Ethan's laugh was scathing. 'You must think I make a habit of courting trouble. Out.' He pointed to the door.

'Can't we even have one last drink together?'

'Gin and tonic?' he mocked.

'If you like.'

'I don't like. Now, go to bed.'

He closed the door with relief. Leaning back against it, he let out a groan of relief. Mentally, physically, he was in agony. He shouldn't even be thinking this way about Savannah. And now he knew she was a virgin he had even less excuse—though how to stop erotic images of her flooding his mind was something he had no answer for. He wanted her. Wanted her? He ached for her. The urge to lose himself in her was overwhelming him, but he couldn't feed on perfection, or drain her innocence to somehow dilute the ugliness inside him.

That was a wound of such long standing he doubted he'd ever be rid of it. It had taken seed in him the day he'd realised his mother had chosen his stepfather over her seven-year-old son, and had germinated on the day she'd seen his bruises in the bath. Instead of questioning them, she had told him she'd take his bike away if he wasn't more careful. Had she really believed the buckle marks on his back had come from a fall? That bitterness was in full flower by the time he'd been ready to make his own way in the world, and those dark secrets had stayed with him. Would he share a legacy like that with Savannah? Not a chance. She was like a ray of light with her whole life in front of her, and he would do anything to protect her. He would do nothing to stop that little candle throwing its beam around the world.

Pulling away from the door, he thrust his hands through his hair with frustration. He wanted Savannah. He wanted to make love to her. The most important thing to him was that Savannah remembered the first time she made love for the right reasons.

He tensed, hearing her footsteps returning. That sound was shortly followed by a tap on the door. 'Yes?'

'Ethan, it's me.'

'What do you want?' He tried to sound gruff. Had she forgotten something? He glanced round the room, already knowing it was a vain hope. He opened the door. She looked like a pale wraith beneath the lights she had insisted on, and they were blazing full in his face. He hardly cared or noticed these days when people turned away from him, but he noticed tonight that Savannah didn't flinch. 'What do you want?' he said wearily.

'You…'

Her voice was so small he couldn't be sure he'd heard her correctly.

'I want you,' she repeated. 'I want you, Ethan.' She held his gaze as she paused, as if she needed to prepare herself for the next step, and then she whispered, 'Will you make love to me?'

He was already closing the door. 'Don't be so silly.'

'I'm not being silly.'

The door was stuck. And then he realised she put her foot in the way. He wanted to laugh at the sight of

Savannah's tiny foot in his door, but, seeing the expression on her face, he knew this was no time for laughter.

'Please, can I come in?' she begged him.

As she looked anxiously up and down the corridor, he knew the answer to that had to be yes. He wouldn't let her make a fool of herself in front of the servants. 'All right,' he agreed, opening the door wide enough for her to slip through. He would soon sort this out. He would tell her it must never happen again and then send her on her way.

But as he closed the door she rounded on him. 'Ethan, what do I have to do to make you see that I'm a woman?'

Noticing Savannah's hands were balled with frustration, he reached out. She reached out too. Whether he intended to hold her off or pull her close, he wasn't sure, he only knew they tangled and collided, and when she closed her eyes he dragged her close and kissed her.

She was trembling like a leaf by the time Ethan pulled away to cup her face and stare into her eyes. This was everything she had ever dreamed of and more. Ethan was everything she had ever dreamed of and more, and his kiss sealed the meeting of two lovers who had to have known each other for longer than one lifetime, and who needed the immediate reassurance of pressing every fragment of their flesh against each other. As she gazed up at Ethan, with all the love she felt for him shining in her eyes, she could have sworn he asked her, 'Are you sure?'

'Yes, I'm sure,' she whispered back.

CHAPTER TEN

HE TASTED heaven when he kissed her. Dipping his head, he kissed her again, deepening the kiss, always acutely conscious that she was so much smaller than he was, and vulnerable—the very thing that held him back.

'Why did you wait so long?' she murmured when he released her.

Because keeping her safe had been paramount. Because he had feared the dark forces inside him might express themselves in contemptuous energy. He should have known Savannah's joyful innocence would defeat them. And now he felt nothing but the desire to cherish her, and to have one night; a night in which he would bring her the ultimate pleasure.

'Ethan?' she prompted, sensing his abstraction.

'I haven't forgotten you,' he murmured, sweeping her into his arms.

Her clothes slipped away in sighs and smothered laughter, and Ethan's kisses drove her remaining fears away as she clung to him, hidden from the world by the spread of his shoulders and the width of his chest. She wasn't even sure how she'd come to be naked, only that she was. And she wasn't embarrassed by that, because

Ethan was there to take care of her, and everything he did or said made her strong. He hadn't even touched her intimately, and yet every part of her was singing with awareness, and she only knew how it felt to soften and melt against him. She clung to him, asking—for what, she hardly knew. She had so much to discover. She had everything to learn.

Ethan carried her across the room to the bed and laid her down on it, where she rested with one arm above her head on a stack of pillows in an attitude of innocent seduction. The linen felt cool and crisp against her raging skin, and she was lost in an erotic haze when she noticed Ethan moving away. 'You're not leaving me?' She sat up.

'This is wrong.'

'What do you mean, "wrong"?' She was blissfully unaware of how nakedly provocative she was to him. 'What's wrong about it?' Now her cheeks were on fire. 'Do you still think I'm too young for you?'

'Correct.' Ethan sounded relieved that she had given him an out. 'Get dressed, Savannah.'

Grabbing his arm, she pushed her face in front of his. 'I won't let you do this.'

'You have no choice.'

'No choice but to be humiliated?' Her voice broke, but Ethan still shook himself free. As he stood looking down at her she thought he had never seemed more magnificent. Or more distant. 'Why?' She opened her arms. 'Why?' she repeated softly. 'Why are you doing this to me, Ethan? Why bring me here at all?'

Because he had thought mistakenly that for one short night he could forget. But the seeds of doubt had been planted deep inside him when his stepfather had assured him in hospital that no one would ever want to look at him again. That message has been driven home when his mother had recoiled from her own child. Was he going to inflict that same horror on Savannah when she saw his others scars? Knowing they were the answer to finishing this, he turned his back so she could see them. The scars on his face were bad enough, but those on his back were truly horrific.

'What are you doing?' she demanded. 'If you expect me to exclaim in horror, you'll be disappointed. These scars make no difference to the way I feel about you.'

'No difference?'

'They don't change what I feel about you in here.'

Savannah's hand rested over her heart. He tried dismissing that with a shrug, but she called him back.

'The damage might be all that others see—but I see you, Ethan.'

'Me?' he mocked unkindly.

'Your scars don't change a thing for me, except that—'

'Yes?' he cut across her, certain now that he must have destroyed her argument.

'They keep us apart,' she finished softly.

Just when Ethan needed her to be strong, she was crying for him, and for what he had lost.

'Dry your face and leave me, Savannah,' he said harshly.

'I'm not going anywhere. Your scars don't frighten me.'

'Then you haven't looked at them properly,' he assured her.

'Oh, but I have,' she argued, seeing inside him more clearly than she ever had before.

'Look at me again,' he suggested in a voice that broke her heart.

There was only one way past this. Kneeling up on the

bed, she reached out while Ethan stood tensely, like a hostile stranger. But little by little the conviction in her eyes drew him to look at her, and she traced his scars with her fingertips, traced the tramlines that criss-crossed his back and which looked as if they had been carved by a serrated knife. She traced each one of them with her eyes and with her fingertips, until she reached his beloved face.

'I revolt you,' he said confidently. 'You don't need to pretend.'

'I don't need to be here at all,' she pointed out. 'Oh, Ethan, you couldn't possibly revolt me. You amaze me.' Ethan's scars would always be a hideous reminder of the cruelty one human being could inflict on another, but they didn't make one jot of difference to the way she felt about him.

'How can I make love to you?' Ethan demanded. 'How?' he repeated with the same passion Savannah had shown him, and when she didn't reply he cupped her chin to make her look at him.

'The usual way?' she suggested softly, and because she loved him so much she risked the ghost of a smile. 'Just don't look to me for any pointers.'

Ethan thought her so cosseted and protected she couldn't tolerate anything that wasn't perfect, when nothing could be further from the truth, Savannah realised as he stripped off his clothes. 'You think my world is all concerts and evening dresses, lace and perfume?' She reached for his hand and laid her cheek against it. 'I was brought up on a farm with straw in my hair, wearing dungarees, and that's where I've always been happiest. I can take reality, Ethan, in rather large doses.'

'So reality like this doesn't trouble you?' Ethan wiped one hand roughly down the scars on his chest.

'Please don't insult me.' As she turned her face up she was aching with the need to wrench the demons out of him. Placing her palms against his chest, she kissed her way slowly across it.

'Don't,' Ethan said, tensing, but she wouldn't stop, and finally he dragged her to him.

Those scars, terrible though they were, didn't even begin to scratch the edges of his power. Ethan was like a gladiator in some ancient etching, wounded but triumphant, and she was hard pressed to think of anything with more sex appeal than that. But inside his heart there was nothing, Savannah's tender inner-self warned her. Yes, she answered back, Ethan's heart was cold, but she had to hope that in time her love would warm him. 'I want you,' she murmured, staring up at him.

'I want you too…more than you know.' And that was true, Ethan realised as he teased Savannah with almost-kisses. She was tender and precious, young and vulnerable, and he would never hurt her. And maybe her innocence was the last hope he had to heal those scars he couldn't reach.

'So, are you coming to bed?' she whispered. Holding his hand, she sank back on the pillows and threw back the covers. 'Don't be shy.'

He laughed. She was so funny and sweet. She had stripped herself bare for him in every way, proving she trusted him, and he would never betray that trust.

As Savannah snuggled lower in the bed, waiting for Ethan, knowing he might change his mind again at any moment, she started having fears on a more practical level. His size alone filled her with apprehension. He must have sensed it, for as he stretched out on the bed at her side he said, 'I think you're nervous.'

'A little,' she admitted, in a shaking voice that betrayed her true feelings.

'There's no need.' He stroked her arm into quivering anticipation, and as she looked into his eyes he promised, 'I would never hurt you, Savannah.'

How could he not? Ethan was so much bigger than the average man—bigger than most men—plus he possessed the power and the stamina of a natural athlete. She'd been around a farm long enough to know that nature allowed for this sort of unlikely coupling, but she wondered now if in some extreme instances such things weren't possible. This was without doubt an extreme instance. She might be plumper than she wanted to be, but she was small and soft compared to Ethan. There was nothing soft about him. He was huge and hard.

Expecting to be soothed and reassured, she was surprised when Ethan moved so quickly to pin her beneath him. And now he was straddling her with his powerful thighs, and she was completely at his mercy while he murmured erotic, outrageous suggestions in her ear that made her squirm with excitement.

'Better?' His lips were curving with amusement as he stared into her eyes.

There was passion in his eyes as well as humour, and she was reassured to a point beyond fear. 'Much better,' she admitted. With Ethan's thighs pressed close against her sides, there was nowhere else on earth she'd rather be. But still she asked for one last reassurance. 'You won't hurt me, will you?'

His answer was to kiss her tenderly until she relaxed, and then he deepened the kiss, which made her want to do anything but relax. Lacing her fingers through Ethan's hair, she tried telling him by her eagerness alone that her nerve endings were screaming for his attention.

'There's a lot more to you than meets the eye, Ms Ross,' Ethan murmured, smiling against her lips.

Savannah stared boldly at Ethan's mouth, shivering with sensation as his kisses migrated down her neck. 'What are you doing?' she asked, writhing with pleasure when he reached the most sensitive hollow above her shoulders.

'Exploring,' Ethan murmured.

The feeling when he teased her nipples was beyond description, and while he suckled and teased the sensation travelled through to the core of her being, until it was impossible to remain still. Ethan could have done whatever he wanted with her, and yet he never once made her feel vulnerable, other than to put her at risk of overdosing on pleasure. Bucking against him, seeking contact, she moved restlessly on the pillows as she assured him, 'I can't take any more of this.'

'So, shall I stop?'

'Just you dare,' she warned him, seeing the laughter in his eyes.

'What's your hurry?' he demanded when she pressed against him.

'You,' Savannah complained fiercely. 'You're my hurry.'

'Then it's time for you to learn a little patience.'

'I don't want to learn patience.' She shivered with delight as he ran his hands down her naked body. 'But, if I do,' she proposed, 'can we do this again?'

'If you're good.'

'I'll be very good,' she assured him. And as he pulled away to look at her she pulled him back. She didn't have sufficient strength to compel Ethan to do anything, but for now the pleasure machine was at her command. 'No more teasing,' she warned him.

'What, then?' His lips were tugging with amusement.

'Make love to me…' And she was deadly serious.

CHAPTER ELEVEN

HE PROTECTED them both, and then touched her in a way he knew she would like. As she moaned beneath him, inviting more of these touches, he feathered kisses down her neck.

He hadn't guessed he could be quite so gentle, or Savannah half so passionate. She brought out the best in him, more than he'd ever known he had, and as she clung to him, crying out his name, moving against him and driving him half-crazy with desire, he held back, knowing he had found someone who could reach him at a level no one else could.

That it should be a young girl like Savannah both surprised him and stirred his conscience. This was the start of a new chapter in Savannah's life as a woman, but when tonight was over he would have to end their relationship. But for now...

Listening to her beating time with her voice to the music of their pleasure, he knew he had never known such extremes of sensation. Gathering her into his arms to stare into her eyes, he brought her to the brink and tipped her over, staying with her through the ecstasy as she enjoyed the release she had been searching for. When she quietened and snuggled in to him, he felt sure as he gazed

FREE BOOKS OFFER

To get you started, we'll send you
2 FREE books and a FREE gift

There's no catch, everything is **FREE**

Accepting your 2 **FREE** books and **FREE** mystery gift
places you under no obligation to buy anything.

Be part of the Mills & Boon® Book Club™ and receive your favourite
Series books up to 2 months before they are in the shops and delivered
straight to your door. Plus, enjoy a wide range of **EXCLUSIVE** benefits!

 Best new women's fiction – delivered right to
your door with FREE P&P

Avoid disappointment – get your books up to
2 months before they are in the shops

No contract – no obligation to buy

We hope that after receiving your free books you'll
want to remain a member. But the choice is yours.
So why not give us a go? You'll be glad you did!

Visit **millsandboon.co.uk** to stay up to date
with offers and to sign-up for our newsletter

2 **FREE** books
and a
FREE gift

P9EI

Mrs/Miss/Ms/Mr   Initials

BLOCK CAPITALS PLEASE

Surname

Address

Postcode

Email

MILLS & BOON®
Pure reading pleasure

MILLS & BOON®
Book Club

FREE BOOK OFFER
FREEPOST CN81
CROYDON
CR9 3WZ

NO STAMP
NEEDED!

NO STAMP
NECESSARY
IF POSTED IN
THE U.K. OR N.I.

into her drowsy face that time was playing tricks on them and that they had known each other much longer than one night. It was a short step from there to knowing Savannah should be with someone who could give her the kind of life she deserved.

'Ethan, where are you?' she murmured, reaching up to touch his face.

'I'm still with you,' he murmured.

'No, you're not,' she argued softly, with barely the strength to open her eyes.

She was right. He was in a dark place he wouldn't take her. Dipping his head, he kissed her deeply, and before she had a chance to question him further he made love to her again.

Savannah lay awake for the rest of the night, pretending to be asleep in the early hours when Ethan left her. She didn't know him well enough to call him back. That struck her as funny and a little embarrassing, because she might not know him but she loved him. And loving him meant she understood his need for space. What had happened between them, what they'd shared, had been so much more than either of them could have expected. Of course, Ethan would need space to consider the changes this must make to his world. The changes to her world were immeasurable. Ethan was her man and her mate, and she had welcomed him inside her body with triumph and excitement. Ethan knew everything about bringing her pleasure, and they had been as one until pleasure had consumed them.

Only one worrying incident had tarnished the night. Ethan had drifted off to sleep after they'd made love, but after a few minutes he had thrown up his hands, as if to ward off a blow. It was some buried memory he couldn't bring himself to share, she guessed, and it hurt her to think of him locked in a nightmare where she couldn't reach him. She had to believe there was a key to breaking that destructive cycle, and that she held that key.

Turning her face into the pillows, Savannah inhaled Ethan's scent. Exhaling softly in the darkness, she turned on her back as contentment consumed her. Her whole being was drenched in a warm, happy glow. She had expected to feel different when she gave herself to a man, but she hadn't expected to feel quite so complete. She couldn't wait to see the same look of happiness in Ethan's eyes, and, as the lilac light of dawn was stealing through the heavy curtains, there was no reason why she shouldn't go and find him.

Stretching her arms, Savannah welcomed the new day with a heart full of joy. It was a new and better world with Ethan in it. She had never believed in love at first sight, but now she did. She'd heard that opposites attracted, and she'd proved that to be right. She was deeply in love, of that there was no doubt, and after last night it couldn't be long before Ethan told her that he loved her too.

He had left Savannah sleeping, and now he was avoiding her at breakfast, choosing instead to start the day with a dawn jog around the extensive grounds surrounding the *palazzo*. But even after that he craved more exercise to clear his mind. He moved on to the gym and after taking an icy shower he swam. As he powered down the Olympic-sized swimming pool there was one thing on his mind: Savannah. He could not get her out of his head.

Did he love her?

The thought was too fantastic to contemplate. He wasn't entitled to love anyone. His stepfather had drummed that into him from the start, and over the years he had come to see that it was the one thing the man had said to him that made sense.

CHAPTER TWELVE

HE DRESSED in the changing rooms just off the swimming pool rather than return to his private suite of rooms where Savannah would still be sleeping. Snapping his watch into position, he prepared to face the day. Heading out of the leisure facility, he made straight for his office. This wasn't a relaxing room where he could watch sport in comfort, but a cold, flickering world where he kept a handle on his business empire. He had this same facility in all his houses. No one was welcome to join him, because this was his techno-version of an ivory tower. He sat in the swivel chair absorbing a blizzard of information, and realised immediately he'd been away too long. He had to go to Savannah now and update her on the current situation. Of course he'd take legal measures to protect her from the braying paparazzi, but the sooner she could leave Italy the sooner she could break free of his shadow and get on with her life.

Savannah ran down the magnificent staircase, consumed by excitement at the thought of seeing Ethan. She could see his servants bustling about in the hallway, and knew that one of them would be able to tell her where he was. She didn't even try to hide her beaming smile, and was half-afraid everyone would guess she was in love with their *gran signore*, and half-afraid they wouldn't. She approached the first young man who smiled back at her to ask him where she could find *Signore* Alexander.

Signore Alexander was in his office as usual, the young man told her, adding that if she would like to wait out on the terrace he would make sure breakfast was served there, and that *Signore* Alexander would be told she was asking for him.

'Thank you!' Savannah exclaimed happily. She must look such a sight, she realised as the young man smiled back at her, but she hadn't wanted to waste a single moment on make-up or drying her hair. After her shower she had quickly thrown on her jeans and a casual top, and left her hair hanging loose and damp down her back. This was a whole new world to her. Catching sight of the housekeeper, she waved, and when the older woman came over to see if Savannah needed anything she took the chance to ask a few discreet questions about the paintings on Ethan's walls. As she expected, the housekeeper told her that Ethan had indeed painted them, but they had never been exhibited as far as the housekeeper could remember.

She'd expected that too, and asked if it would be possible to open more windows. 'And I'd like to pick some flowers, if that's all right. I'd love to fill the *palazzo* with flowers—if I'm allowed to.'

'*Signorina*, we have a hothouse full of flowers—and that's before you even start on the garden—but no one ever picks them.'

'Oh, perhaps I shouldn't.' It wasn't her house, after all, and she'd made enough changes.

'Perhaps you should,' the housekeeper encouraged. 'Why don't I show you where the vases are kept?'

'Are you sure Signore Alexander won't mind?'

'I'm sure the *palazzo* can only benefit from your attentions, *signorina*.'

With her fresh flowers newly arranged in the centre of the table, Savannah settled herself at the breakfast table on the terrace to wait for Ethan. Last night was still framed in a rosy glow. Her world had been turned upside down over the past twenty-four hours, and it was a very beautiful world indeed, Savannah thought as she gazed across the emerald parkland. There was a lake at the *palazzo*, as well as formal gardens, and with wooden shutters framing the sparkling windows and vivid bougainvillea tumbling down the walls, the ancient palace was like something out of her most romantic fantasy.

Savannah's gaze returned to the floral arrangement on the table. She had picked the flowers herself and had placed them in a vase. It wasn't much of a gift, on the scale of the things Ethan owned, but it was a love token given with sincerity.

'It's good to see you've made yourself at home.'

'Ethan!' In her euphoric state it seemed to Savannah she only had to think of Ethan for him to appear. 'You startled me,' she admitted, still clutching her chest. She sank down in her chair again, not wanting him to think her too excitable—or, worst-case scenario, too much in love with him. If he thought that it might prompt the unwanted opinion that she was too young to know what she wanted yet.

'I didn't mean to startle you. Perhaps you were daydreaming?'

'Perhaps I was,' she admitted shyly.

'No reason why you shouldn't. I want you to enjoy your short stay here.'

Savannah paled at Ethan's mention of a short stay. So last night had meant nothing to him. Of course it hadn't meant anything to him, Savannah realised, breaking up inside. Ethan was a sophisticated man, and she was...

What? A fool?

She was a farm girl from the depths of the country. And perhaps that was where she should have stayed.

She had jumped to so many conclusions, and all of them wrong. This man was not the tender lover from last night, but a stern and formidable stranger who was currently staring back at her as if she were a visitor he barely knew, and whom he was kindly putting up for the night.

'Do you have everything you need?' he said.

Not nearly, Savannah thought, following Ethan's gaze to her empty plate. 'I was waiting for you.'

'There's no need.' He appeared restless, as if he didn't even want to sit down.

'Is something wrong?' she asked him.

'I need to speak to you.' His voice, his manner, was a return to their former, professional relationship.

'It's not my parents, is it?' That at least would make a horrible sort of sense.

'No. They're both well,' he reassured her. He reached out a hand that didn't quite make it to her shoulder. 'Do you mind if I sit down, Savannah?'

Did she mind? It was the wrong question from the right mouth. 'Of course I don't mind.' Her heart squeezed tight. She was tense all over. 'Would you like some tea? Can I pour it for you?'

'I don't want anything, thank you.'

Normal, everyday things should make a crisis manageable, shouldn't they? It didn't work for her. Ethan hadn't even glanced at the flowers she'd picked for him. and now she braced herself, certain there was worse to come.

'The paparazzi are at the gates, Savannah.'

How right she was! 'Here at the *palazzo*?' She couldn't believe it. The stab of distress she felt at the thought that Ethan's privacy had been breached, and that it was all her fault, was terrible.

'You mustn't be alarmed,' he said, misreading her expression.

'Alarmed? I'm concerned for you.'

Ethan wasn't listening. 'If you stay in the grounds and let me handle them, you'll be safe. Savannah,' he said, staring at her intently, 'Trust me. I won't let them near you.'

All the ground she'd gained had been lost. Ethan thought she couldn't handle it. He was going to mop up the mess she'd created without her help. No wonder he'd cooled towards her. He'd had time to think, and had concluded she was a liability. A man who guarded his privacy as Ethan did must be eager to be rid of her. 'I can't tell you how sorry I am.'

'Sorry?' he cut across her. 'Please don't be. You have nothing to apologise for, Savannah. You've done nothing wrong.'

Other than to fall in love with him. Ethan was all concern for her—not because he loved her, but because she was under his protection—and he would do anything it took to keep her safe. Savannah knew she shouldn't want more than that, but she did. 'What can I do to help?'

'Stay out of the way?' Ethan suggested.

So she was to be compliant, invisible and ineffectual? She had never longed for the farm more. At least there she could have shown Ethan another side of her. It seemed now that was a side of her he would never see.

'The only problem, as I see it,' he observed, thoughtfully thumbing his stubble, 'Is that you'll have to stay here a little longer.'

He couldn't have made it clearer. There never had been any long-term plans where Ethan was concerned. That was the price she must pay for playing the game of love without the necessary credentials. 'But I can't just sit here. I have to do something.'

'The best thing you can do,' he said, 'is stay out of my way.'

Ethan was right; what did she know? Life on a working farm was great, but it wasn't the best apprenticeship for this world of celebrity. Whatever Ethan did now would be swift and decisive. He'd deal with the press and then he'd come back for her, by which time she must be ready to leave.

He returned to his office where he immediately contacted his legal team. He wanted them to draft an injunction to keep Savannah safe and free from harassment by the press when she left him, which must be soon now. She preoccupied his thoughts, and he missed her already. He'd noticed the softening touches she'd made—the dust sheets had all been removed and the *palazzo* had been thoroughly aired. There were flower arrangements in many of the rooms, punctuating the ancient artefacts and imbuing the *palazzo* with fresh life, he reflected, tapping his pen on the table top as he waited for his call to connect.

He had to stop this! He was relieved when his call connected, and he heard the cool, impersonal voice of his lawyer on the other end. Savannah was a real danger to the status quo in his life. She had made him look at things that had never mattered to him before—frescoes, carvings, and all the incredible paintings he'd inherited when he'd bought the *palazzo*. She was a Salome of the arts, he concluded, whilst firing instructions at his lawyer. Savannah had beguiled him with her voice, and then enchanted him with her innocence and naivety, tempting him beyond the logical and factual to appreciate the beauty and emotional wealth locked in the treasures he owned. Raking his hair into a worse state of disorder than before, he signed off, determined that Savannah's qualities would never be compromised. Thank goodness he'd recognised in time the imperative of putting a stop to this fantasy of loving her, and had brought cool legal minds to bear on the problem instead.

A few short words and his lawyer had got the picture. In fact, his lawyer had seen all the pictures. As he stowed the phone, he relaxed. Back in a familiar world without emotion, he could focus on the facts. Savannah's welfare meant everything to him. His feelings towards her might have muddied the water for a short time, but that was over now.

Over…

He still had her music. Picking up the remote-control, he turned on her CD. As Savannah's voice floated around him he found it impossible to remain tense—impossible to forget how very special she was, and how at all costs he must protect her.

At *all* costs, he reminded himself, as he left the room to make sure that Savannah had the chance to live her dream.

She wasn't good with make-up. In fact, she was useless, Savannah concluded as she peered into the mirror. She was back in her room and, having packed, she supposed putting on make-up before she left was all about pride. She was going to leave the *palazzo* with her head held high, and not looking like some washed-out waif. But a good technique with make-up took more skill than she had. Professional make-up artists had worked on her for the photo shoot for her album, though when she appeared on stage she could pile on the slap with the best of them; no subtlety required. But she hardly ever wore make-up off-duty. It would frighten the animals, she concluded wryly.

Well, she would just have to do, Savannah decided, having pulled her face this way and that. With no outfits to choose from, she was wearing jeans and flip-flops. But at least she had combed her hair, and she was wearing the pretty, lacy cardigan she always packed to wear over her evening gown to keep her warm in the wings while she was waiting to sing.

Moistening her lips, she attempted a pout and quickly gave up. You could put the glitz into the farm girl, but you could never take the farm girl out of Savannah Ross.

And thank goodness for it. She'd need every bit of grit she had to part from Ethan and act as if it didn't hurt like hell.

After instructing his lawyers, Ethan went outside and issued a statement to the press. He went back to the office, and had barely walked through the door when he saw Savannah's face staring out of one of the monitors. It was so unexpected, he stood transfixed, and then realised one of the reporters had somehow managed to elude his security staff and had accosted Savannah as she was coming out of the bedroom on her way across the court-yard. She was going to say goodbye to his staff in a typical act of kindness, he realised. His eyes narrowed as he took in the scene. Far from running scared, Savannah had the news hound by the elbow and was showing him the door. From the tilt of her chin he gathered she was about to send the man off with a flea in his ear. But were more opportunists hanging around? He was already through the door, this time with a look of murder in his eyes.

One reporter she could handle, but a jostling crowd…

CHAPTER THIRTEEN

HE WAS mobbed the moment he stepped outside the door by the paparazzi. Now that they'd seen Savannah leaving his private rooms, he would struggle to deny that anything was going on between them. Whatever Savannah had told them must have been good, he concluded as the reporters formed an arc around him. He gave them a look and they went scattering back. They had agreed to leave, and had been caught out. The photographers remained a safe distance away from him, hovering like slavering hyenas as they bumped each other shamelessly in an attempt to capture both him and Savannah in the same frame. He hadn't looked at her directly yet, but he was deeply conscious of her standing close by him. He made no attempt to close the gap. He had no intention of compromising her, and would keep his distance until he'd had his say.

'Is it true you and Ms Ross are an item?' one of them asked. 'I thought you told us that Ms Ross's welfare was your only concern.'

So, what had she told them? He had no way of knowing. His only concern was to protect Savannah and prevent scandal blighting her career. They had spent the whole day avoiding just this situation—but when she gave him a look that said her brave act of ejecting the reporter from the palace grounds had gone badly wrong, and she was sure she had just shot her reputation to hell and back, he moved swiftly into damage-limitation mode. He had two options: he could deny a relationship, and make Savannah look like a fool if she had said something different, or confirm one and bring her firmly under his protection. There was really no decision to be made. As he strolled over to her an air of expectancy swept the reporters, and as they fell back he put his arm around Savannah's shoulders.

For a moment Savannah couldn't get her head round the fact that Ethan was standing next to her. And not just standing at her side, but supporting her. The shock of feeling his arm around her shoulders must have gummed up her brain, she concluded as he gave her a reassuring squeeze. She knew this must just be an act for the benefit of the press, but it was a pretty seductive fantasy.

'I never saw you as a security-guard before, Ms Ross,' Ethan murmured. 'But you handle yourself pretty well.'

Savannah felt a rush of pride and relief as she identified the reporter she'd firmly ushered out of the grounds standing in line with the others. They were quite a team, she thought wryly as Ethan dealt effortlessly with the hail of questions—much good it would do her as far as her non-existent romance with Ethan was concerned!

'One question at a time, ladies and gentlemen, please.' Ethan raised his free hand to bring everyone to order, and she noticed how his relaxed tone of voice set everyone at ease.

'I'll answer all your questions. At least—' Ethan tempered with a glint in his eyes '—those I am prepared to.'

This made the reporters laugh, and as Ethan turned to glance at Savannah she felt her body respond. 'Of course, I can't speak for Ms Ross,' he added, with another of those dangerously addictive, reassuring squeezes.

As the noise of conversation fell Savannah realised how tense she had become. Pressed up hard against Ethan, she had grown as stiff as a board. Ethan, of course, had no such inhibitions, and was perfectly relaxed in the spotlight. He felt great—fantastic, in fact—warm, strong and in control. The first surprise he launched was to announce that she had his full authority to say anything she wanted to say about their relationship.

Their relationship?

'Not that Ms Ross needs my authority to do so,' he added with an engaging shrug. 'She's got plenty to say for herself.' Ethan's eyes were darkly amused as he turned to her for confirmation. He went on to agree to answer three questions. After which he was sure they'd all want to get away. 'So choose wisely,' he added, which brought another chuckle from the crowd.

He'd got them in the palm of his hand, Savannah realised. The female reporters were practically panting to be first to ask him questions. They might as well have called out, 'Choose me! Choose me!' she thought tensely as a forest of red-gloss-tipped hands shot up. How were they supposed to resist Ethan's wicked smile when it was sending seismic signals through her own system? And something told her this was just the tip of the iceberg where Ethan's charm offensive was concerned.

So, was she jealous? And since when? Since she realised she couldn't have him. She might not be able to have him, but did she want other women going there?

Now she was supposed to convince him she knew this was only an act for the press. Well, she'd give it her best shot.

The first question came from a young woman, who moistened her lips and arranged them in a pout before asking him, 'So, do you deny there is a relationship between yourself and your protégée, Ethan?'

'Not at all,' he said. 'Why should I?'

'But Ms Ross said—'

He didn't even blink, though he couldn't have had a clue what she had said. 'Miss Ross was trying to protect me...' As Ethan turned to look at her and his voice softened, his eyes held everything she could have hoped for.

Except sincerity, Savannah registered, meeting Ethan's gaze and holding it so that he was in no doubt that she knew this was all pretence. He got the message loud and clear. There was more humour in his gaze than anything else— humour and warmth—which was a devastating combination in such a dark, forbidding man, and all the warning she needed to keep her feelings for Ethan in check.

'So you and Ms Ross *are* an item?' the same girl pressed.

'Take care.' Ethan cut in like this was a game. 'That's your second question. Don't you think you should give someone else a chance?'

Reluctantly, the girl stepped back.

'*Are* you and Ms Ross an item?' A well-known wily reporter from a national television-station asked the same question, with more relaxed laughter.

'Ms Ross has already given you her answer—and, before you ask me to confirm what she's said, please think about your stories and how you're going to flesh them out. The tycoon leaving the stadium with his star performer can only be old news now, right?'

Ethan's audacity made Savannah gasp. Was he going

to write the press release for the reporters? From hunted to hunter in the space of a few seconds was not bad going, she reflected, even as the wily reporter pressed his lips down in acknowledgement of a worthy foe. 'But you must admit it's a great headline?' he said, launching his own fishing expedition.

'Is that question two or three?' Ethan's eyes were glinting with challenge, and Savannah knew he was enjoying this. Everything was a game to Ethan, a game he was determined to win.

'Will Ms Ross be staying at the *palazzo* with you for long?' The reporter waited patiently for Ethan to reply while the rest held a collective breath.

'As long as she likes,' Ethan said, turning to look at Savannah when she started to protest.

Okay, so she was only trying to defend Ethan's dignity—forget her honour; he clearly had. Pulling her tight, Ethan kissed away her protest, leaving her trembling like a leaf and everyone else gasping. 'Which means Miss Ross might be here quite some time,' he announced.

By the time Ethan released her she was fit for nothing, and even the reporters were still reeling with surprise that the famous recluse had come out. Ethan, of course, was completely unmoved, and continued his verbal jousting as if nothing unusual had happened.

So, what was he was up to? Disarming the press with more truth than they could handle? Even she wasn't naïve enough to believe that. His behaviour towards her had to be an act. She should have known better than to try and fight Ethan's battles in his own back yard. He was hardly the type to let her take over.

As cameras swivelled to take a better shot of her, Savannah's arms flew up instinctively to shield her face, and in that same moment Ethan stepped in front of her. 'We have a deal,' he told everyone firmly. 'And I expect you to honour that agreement, as I shall. I answer your questions, and in return you respect our privacy.'

Ethan's back cut off Savannah's view of the proceedings, but her pulse pounded a reminder that Ethan was a warrior who wouldn't allow her to stand alone. That didn't mean he felt the same about her as she felt about him, just that he was a natural born protector. She longed to tell the press that, whatever the future held for them, she adored Ethan Alexander and always would.

'And your third and last question?' Ethan prompted, reclaiming Savannah's attention as he drew her close.

'How long do you expect this *liaison* to last, Ethan?' the reporter asked him, making the word liaison sound sordid.

Savannah felt Ethan's grip change and soften, instead of growing angry, and she realised that she could have walked away from him at that point, had she wanted to.

'Don't you think it would be more chivalrous if you addressed that question to Ms Ross?' Ethan's tone was neutral, almost as if he was condoning the reporter's scathing tone. But as the reporter turned to her Savannah felt very strongly that Ethan had played some clever move.

'Well, Ms Ross?' the reporter demanded.

Before she could answer, Ethan held up his hand. 'You've had your three questions,' he pointed out wryly.

As a clamour of protest threatened to break out, Ethan smiled at her. 'Why don't we pose for an official photograph?' he suggested.

'Are you serious?' Savannah said incredulously, still reeling from Ethan's killer move.

'Never more so.'

As Ethan's mouth quirked with familiar humour,

Savannah realised she trusted him. It was that simple and that complicated, she thought, taking her place standing at Ethan's side.

That was the signal for the photographers to rush to grab the best positions. They called for them to look this way and that, and fortunately smiling came easily to her. It wasn't that hard to pretend she felt good pressed up close to Ethan, and when the photographers asked them to change position, and he brought her in front of him with his arms loosely slung around her waist, she could have happily stayed there for ever. How hard could it be to rest her head against the chest of the man she loved with all her heart?

'There's just one more thing, ladies and gentlemen of the press,' Ethan announced when everyone had had their fill of them. 'And my lawyers have mailed this informa-tion to your editors,' he added. 'My legal team has drafted an injunction protecting Ms Ross. It was placed in front of a judge this morning. Everything that falls outside what I have told you will be jumped on. And, of course, this order will protect Ms Ross when she leaves here and picks up her career. She will not be harassed or there will be legal consequences. She will be left alone.'

He didn't need to say more, Savannah realised, taking in everyone's expression. There wasn't one reporter there who was prepared to risk an expensive libel case that might put their job in jeopardy. Ethan had acted swiftly and effectively to protect her.

'But you've told us very little,' the wily older reporter complained. 'Other than the fact that what we have on you and Ms Ross is old news.'

As they looked at each other both men knew this was the end game. There was nothing left for the reporters to do but to pack up and leave. They did so without further comment, but as they reached their vehicles the older reporter turned and tipped his head in Ethan's direction, as if acknowledging another man at the top of his game.

'With the lives we both lead, it's almost inevitable that our paths will cross again,' Ethan explained as they watched the reporter walk away.

'And you don't mind that?'

'Challenge always gives me a buzz.'

So Ethan's life would go flat now. And she hadn't been much of a challenge for him, had she? Savannah reflected, remembering she'd practically begged Ethan to make love to her.

His phone rang and he had to turn away to take the call. 'Will you excuse me?' he said politely.

Savannah waited.

'The England manager,' Ethan revealed, sounding pleased. 'The boys won their match and would like to come over for a celebration.'

'Oh, that's great news!'

He looked at her sternly. 'I was about to say, but—'

'But what?' Savannah cut in again.

'But, in case you hadn't noticed, I don't do entertaining.' Having slipped the phone into the pocket of his shirt, Ethan started walking back towards the *palazzo*.

'But I do,' Savannah called after him recklessly.

'You do what?'

Ethan stopped so abruptly, she almost ran into him again. 'I do entertaining,' Savannah explained, staying a safe distance away. 'In fact, I love entertaining.' The prospect of humiliation was very real, seeing as she was supposed to be leaving the *palazzo*, not arranging a party for Ethan. But what did she have to lose? 'So, if you need a hostess, you've got one.'

'No.' Ethan quickened his step.

'No?' Prompted into action, Savannah ran after him. 'Why not?'

'For the obvious reasons.'

'What obvious reasons? Ethan, please, just wait and listen to me.'

'I said no, Savannah. Thank you for the offer, but there isn't going to be a party here. Half the *palazzo* is shut up. It hasn't seen the light of day since I bought it.'

'Well, what a good excuse to open it up. It can be done, Ethan, just like my room.'

Shaking his head, he strode away from her. 'I've got business appointments.'

'I could handle everything for you.'

'You?' He didn't break stride as he headed back towards the *palazzo*.

'Yes, me,' Savannah said patiently, scurrying along at his side.

'The boys can come over for a quiet kitchen-supper.' She felt like punching the air.

'But I don't do celebrations.'

'There's always a first time.'

'That's a popular misconception put about by an optimist,' Ethan informed her, speeding up again.

'You wouldn't even have to be there,' Savannah added hastily, forced to run to keep up as they crossed the court-yard. 'Unless you wanted to be there, of course,' she added, seeing Ethan's expression darken.

'If I agree to anything at all, it will be a quiet meal organised by my staff. And an early night for everyone,' he told her sternly, reaching for the door.

'Oh…I'm sure the squad will enjoy that.' Savannah pulled a face Ethan couldn't see as he lifted the latch on the big wooden door that led through to the utility rooms at the back of the *palazzo*.

'So, what are you saying?' He swung round to confront her. 'You want to stay another night?'

It would have been nice if he'd wanted her to. She swallowed her pride. 'If it would help you, yes; I'm prepared to do that.'

Ethan's hum told her nothing, his expression even less, but she wasn't done yet. This was one straw she wasn't going to lose her grip on. 'You helped me. I'd like to help you.' She gave a nonchalant shrug. 'It's the least I can do.'

The very least.

CHAPTER FOURTEEN

'My staff won't need your help with a kitchen-supper,' Ethan pointed out.

'I'd like to do a little more than that for the squad.' And when Ethan threw her a hard stare she added, 'Don't look so suspicious, Ethan. I'm not going to turn it into a bacchanalian romp.'

'I should hope not.' He held the door into the hallway for her.

'Just some good food and hospitality.'

'A kitchen-supper,' Ethan confirmed, which wasn't what Savannah had in mind at all. There was that cobwebby old dining-room to be brought out of wraps, just for starters.

'Either way,' she said, curbing her enthusiasm as more ideas came to her, 'we should consult with your staff first, as this is very short notice for them.'

'At the start of this discussion, tonight wasn't going to be an event my staff would need notice for,' he pointed out.

True, but she had learned when to speak and when to say nothing—and what was it people said about actions speaking louder than words?

* * *

She wasn't going to build any bridges with marshmallow and fluff, Savannah reflected, rolling up her sleeves to help Ethan's staff prepare the neglected dining-room. Beneath the dust sheets the furniture was still beautiful, and the upholstery, in a variety of jewel-coloured silks, was as good as new. Ethan had carved his own narrow path through the glories of the *palazzo*, looking neither left nor right, she guessed, until he'd reached the suite of rooms he had chosen to occupy.

Later that day as Savannah straightened up to survey the finished dining-room she joined Ethan's staff in exclaiming with delight. The transformation from spooky and dark to glittery and bright was incredible. But would Ethan share their pleasure, or would he be furious? Having given his tacit consent to a quiet evening in, he would hardly have expected her to expand that brief quite so radically. But the old *palazzo* deserved an airing and the England squad certainly deserved this.

Savannah thanked each member of the household by name before they left the dining-room, knowing she couldn't have done any of this without them. She had been accepted by the people who worked for Ethan, and their smiles were so warm and friendly that she felt quite at home. Which was a joke, because this was not her home. In twenty-four hours she would fly back to England and never see it again. That was her deadline for convincing Ethan that this scene of warmth, comfort and welcome didn't have to end when she left, and that it was better for everyone who lived in the *Palazzo dei Tramonti Dorati* than cobwebs, shadows and dust.

Taking one last look around before she left the glowing

room, Savannah thought of this as her one chance to give Ethan an evening to remember, as well as to restore the heart of his *palazzo* before she returned home.

Ethan's chef excelled himself, working non-stop in the kitchen, and when the housekeeper had finished lighting all the candles Savannah thought she had never seen a lovelier room. With its soaring ceiling and deep, mullioned windows, the flicker of candlelight, the long, oval dining-table dressed with fine linen, sparkling crystal glasses, and Ethan's best silver cutlery brought out of storage for the occasion, it looked quite magnificent. Ethan had sent a message to say he had been detained on business and to start without him. What he would think of her opening up the dining-room when he was expecting to hunker down in the kitchen, she could only guess. It wouldn't be good news for her, Savannah thought, but what mattered more was that Ethan saw the possibilities here. There was a palpable air of excitement amongst his staff, and at their urging she had even gone mad and donned her neglected pink gown for the evening.

Feeling a flutter of excitement at the thought that all that was missing now were the guests, Savannah slowly turned full circle one last time to take everything in.

He was annoyed at being late, but it couldn't be helped. The meeting had run on longer than he'd thought. The England squad was already here. He'd seen their coach in the courtyard. He could hear the sound of male laughter as he strode across the hall. He ran up to his room to shower and change, eager to get back down and support Savannah. There was too much testosterone floating around for his liking. It was only on his way downstairs again that he realised the sounds he could hear were not coming from the kitchen, but from the dining-room. He frowned as he retraced his steps across the hall. The room had been shut up for years…

A manservant opened the double doors for him with a flourish, and as he stood on the threshold he was momentarily stunned. The scene laid out in front of him showed the oak-panelled dining-room fully restored to its former glory. It was a haven of colour and warmth, and the sound of fun and laughter drew him in.

If Savannah had chosen to be a theatrical designer rather than a singer, she couldn't have conjured up a more glamorous set. But in the centre of that set was the centre of his attention: Savannah, looking more dazzling than he'd ever seen her.

Looking…There were no words to describe how Savannah looked. With her soft, golden curls hanging loose in a shimmering curtain down her back, she looked ethereal, and yet glamorous and womanly. She was playing hostess to the squad in a stunning pale-pink gown that fitted her voluptuous figure perfectly. This was no child, or some wanton sex-kitten displaying her wares in front of a roomful of men. This was a real woman, a woman with class, with heart and light in her eyes, a woman he now remembered was accustomed to working alongside men on her parents' farm, which explained her ease of manner. That was what made it so easy for his friends on the squad to relate to her, he realised.

'Ethan…'

Seeing him, her face lit up, and as she came towards him he realised he had expected to be shunned after the churlish way he'd treated her, but instead she was holding out her hands to invite him in. She was more than beautiful, he realised in that moment; Savannah was one of those rare people: a force for good.

'Come,' she said softly. 'Come and meet your guests, Ethan.'

His attention was centred on her after that moment, and though he was quickly immersed in the camaraderie of the team he was acutely aware of her every second.

The boys in the squad laughed goodnaturedly, and made him admit that what Savannah had organised for them was a whole lot better than a quiet kitchen-supper. He agreed, and eventually even he was laughing. What Savannah had done for the team had made them feel special. She made him feel special.

It thrilled Savannah to see what an inspiration Ethan was to the younger players. Everyone showed him the utmost respect. At Ethan's insistence she was sitting next to him. She couldn't bear to think this was the last occasion when she would do that.

'Here's to England winning the Six Nations,' he said, standing up to deliver the toast. 'And here's to the only one amongst us without a broken nose.'

It took Savannah a moment to realise Ethan was raising his glass to her, and as everyone laughed and cheered he added, 'To our gracious hostess for the evening, the lovely Savannah Ross.'

'Savannah Ross!' the squad chorused, raising their glasses to her.

Savannah's cheeks were crimson, but Ethan hadn't finished with her yet. 'Would you sing for us?' he murmured discreetly. As his warm breath brushed her cheeks her heart beat even faster. She was touched by the request, but terrified at the thought of singing in front of a room full of people, all of whose faces she could see quite clearly. There was no nice, safe barrier of blinding footlights to hide behind here.

'I'm sure you don't want to hear my rendition of Rusalka's *Song to the Moon*!' She laughed, as if the aria's romantic title would be enough to put him off.

But Ethan wasn't so easily dissuaded. 'That sounds lovely.' He looked round the table for confirmation, and everyone agreed.

As the room went still, Savannah wondered could she do this? Could she sing the song of the water-sprite telling the moon of her love for one man? And could she do that with Ethan staring at her?

Help him in dreams to think of me...

'No pressure,' Ethan said dryly.

Pressing her fingertips on the table, she slowly got up.

Silvery moon in the great, dark sky...

Savannah hardly remembered what happened after the opening line, because she was lost in the music and the meaning of the words. She didn't come to until she heard everyone cheering and banging the table. And then she found Ethan at her side. 'Did I—?'

'Sing beautifully?' he said, staring deep into her eyes. 'Yes, you did.'

She relaxed and, laughing as she shook her head in exaggerated complaint, raised her eyes to the ceiling for the benefit of the squad. 'What can you do with him?'

'What can *you* do with him?' Ethan murmured, but when her quick glance brushed his face she saw his expression hadn't changed. It was always so hard to know what Ethan was thinking.

'Our only difficulty with Ethan,' one of the players told her, 'is that he refuses to consider anything that has his name, a team, a ball, and a rugby pitch in the same sentence.'

'Leave it,' Ethan warned goodnaturedly when he overheard this comment.

Savannah kept her thoughts to herself. But didn't everyone know Ethan's injuries had prevented him from further involvement in the game? He just couldn't risk one of the man-mountains landing on top of him. Tactfully, she changed the subject. Tapping her water glass with a spoon, she offered to sing an encore if the boys would help her with the chorus. And as she'd hoped that soon took the spotlight off Ethan.

After murdering every song they could think of, the players retired to bed, while Savannah insisted on changing and staying behind to help the staff clear up. 'It's late,' she told Ethan, 'and everyone's tired. We've had a wonderful evening, thanks to your staff working so late, so I'm going to stay and help them.'

'Then so will I,' he said, giving his staff the night off.

'I never thought I'd have the courage to sing in front of such a small group of people,' Savannah admitted as they worked side by side, putting the room to rights.

'You could certainly see the whites of their eyes,' he agreed wryly.

But none of them had eyes as beautiful as Ethan's, Savannah mused, keeping this thought in a warm little pocket close to her heart. 'You gave me the courage to do it,' she admitted.

'Then I'm pleased if your short stay here has helped your confidence.'

Savannah didn't hear any more. The warm little pocket shrivelled to nothing. She'd been trying to tell Ethan they were a great team, but it had fallen on deaf ears. And if that was all he thought this incredible time had meant to her she really was on a hiding to nothing. But at least she could stop worrying whether she had given away too much, singing her impassioned song to the moon, Savannah reflected sadly, for just as Ethan's talent for inspiring people and for his art was wasted so was her love for him.

'You were great tonight,' he said, reclaiming her attention as he toed open the door to carry a tray to the kitchen. But just as her heart began to lift, he added, 'I'm really glad we signed you, Savannah Ross.'

She was still flat when Ethan returned with the empty tray. 'Well, have we finished?' he said.

'Looks like it,' Savannah agreed, checking round. 'What?' she prompted when Ethan continued to look at her.

She would ignore that look of his. Memories of their love-making sent an electric current shooting through her body; she'd ignore that too. What she must do was leave the room. 'Excuse me, please.' She avoided Ethan's gaze as she tried to move past him.

'I thought you might want a nightcap.' One step was all it took to block her way.

That was the cue for her willpower to strike. She wanted Ethan to make love to her one last time, though in her heart she knew sex would never be enough; she wanted more; she wanted all of him.

But, if sex was all they had, what then?

CHAPTER FIFTEEN

'IT DOESN'T usually take you so long to decide, Savannah.'

True, Savannah accepted wryly. The way Ethan had pitched his voice, so low and sexy, was sending her desire for him into overdrive. 'Water's fine.'

What was she doing? So much for her intention to retire to bed and think chaste thoughts! She'd sold out for a glass of water, and now Ethan showed no signs of moving out of her way.

He wanted her. He loved her. Savannah had impressed him tonight in every way, but what he felt for her was so much more than pride in her achievements. She had filled his home with light and laughter, and he could never thank her enough for that. She'd worked as hard as any member of his staff to make his friends feel welcome. She'd mixed well with the men and had known where the boundaries lay and how to impose a few of her own without causing embarrassment. She'd told him more about the farm and her life there, and he only wished he'd had the chance to see it before their lives diverged. But at least she was leaving on a high note. He would never forget the way that men with battered faces had treated her like a favourite sister, and how much trouble she had gone to for them. And how she had looked so beautiful, and yet not once had flaunted her appeal. In fact, quite the opposite; she seemed totally unaware of it.

'It was a great night, Ethan; let's not spoil it now.'

'Spoil it?' he queried.

'You know I have to go tomorrow.'

So let's not draw this out, she was telling him. And, yes, he should let her go. 'It was a very good night,' he agreed, fighting back passion. But there were forces inside him that overruled his modern take on the situation. She was his. He wanted her. He loved this woman. The desire to possess Savannah overwhelmed him, and as she sensed the change in him and her eyes darkened he dragged her into his arms.

This was wrong. This was fool's gold. This was also the only thing on earth she wanted right now. She put up a token resistance, pressing her hands against Ethan's chest, but as she stared into his eyes and he murmured something decidedly erotic she gave in. Ethan understood the needs of her body and how to turn her on in every way there was. He knew how to extend her pleasure until she was mad with it, mad for him, and now all expectations of sleeping alone and dreaming chaste thoughts were gone. She groaned softly as he teased her with his lips, and with his tongue and teeth, reminding her of what came next. He felt so hard, toned and warm as his hands found her breasts. And he tasted of warm, hungry man— clean, so good, and so very familiar. And she'd missed him in the few hours they'd been apart.

But she shouldn't… They mustn't…

Her hips were already tilting, thrusting, inviting, while

Ethan was backing her relentlessly towards the door. She waited until he slipped the lock before lacing her fingers through his thick dark hair and making him her prisoner. 'Shall we be captives here for long?'

'As long as it takes,' he promised huskily.

And as he brushed her lips with his mouth, and she sighed and melted, she murmured, 'Kiss me.'

'Since when do I have to be prompted?'

Since never. Savannah purred with desire, and then gasped as Ethan swept her into his arms and carried her across the room. 'What do you think you're doing?' she murmured as he laid her down on the rug.

'A nice, soft rug is so much kinder than a table, don't you think?'

Savannah's cheeks blazed red as she understood Ethan's intentions were to take her any place, any time, anywhere, much as her fantasies had dictated. 'Why didn't I think of the rug?' she murmured, arcing towards him.

'Because you've still got a lot to learn?'

'Everything,' she corrected him happily.

'So, I'll teach you. Where would you like me to start?'

'Right here…' She placed his hand over her breast, and uttered a happy cry when he turned her beneath him.

Holding her wrists loosely above her head, Ethan dealt with the fastening on her clothes. She loved it when his big, warm hands cupped her buttocks, subjecting her to delicious stroking moves as he prepared her. She loved to feel those hands caressing and supporting her as he positioned her. She loved everything about him—the wide spread of his shoulders, the power in his chest, and the biceps flexing on his arms when he braced himself above her. She felt protected and loved. She wanted this, needed him—needed Ethan deep inside her so she could forget she had to leave him in the morning. Wrapped up in passion, she wound her legs around him and lost herself again.

His intention had been to take Savannah to bed and make love to her all night, but here, in front of a crackling fire in the candlelit room she had made beautiful, there were all the romantic elements she could wish for, and he wanted to give her the full fairy-tale romance. All that had ever stood in the way of that was his cold, unfeeling heart, but for tonight he had the chance to hold Savannah in his arms while she slept, and he wanted to remember how she felt in his arms, and how she looked when he held her safe. He wanted to keep her safe always. *Safe from him.*

He knew what he must do, Ethan accepted grimly. Easing his arm out from under her, he kissed Savannah awake like some prince in a distorted fairy-tale. There could be no happy ending here. She smiled at him groggily. Reaching for his hand, she brought it to her lips. As she gazed at him her lips moved, and the dread that she was going to say 'I love you' made him kiss her again, but this time not to wake her, but to silence her. He wouldn't lure her into his cold, dark world, but the moment he released her she asked the one question he had been dreading most. 'Ethan, tell me about your scars.'

He turned his face away for a moment, cursing his arrogant assumption that Savannah could ever be distracted from her purpose. She touched his face to bring him back to her, but he pulled away. 'What do you want to know?' he said coldly.

'Everything.'

Everything? The word echoed in his head. If he would

save her from him, he was blindingly certain he would save her from *everything*.

'Ethan, why is it so wrong for me to want to be close to you when we just made love? I want to know who did this to you and why. Surely you can trust me enough to tell me that?'

She had no idea. How could she? He removed himself a little more, both physically and mentally. 'I can understand your fascination.' He spoke in a murmur as he reasoned it through, his mind set on other occasions when he'd suspected the questioner had obtained some sort of foul, vicarious thrill out of the violence.

'Fascination?' Savannah's voice called him back. 'Ethan, you don't know me at all. How can you think me so shallow?'

'Aren't all women shallow?' The bitterness burst out of him before he could stop it.

'I don't know what kind of women you've met in the past,' Savannah countered hotly. 'And I don't want to. But I can assure you I'm *not* shallow.' Her voice was raised, her body tense, and her gaze held his intently—but after a moment she froze, and a change came over her. 'Is your mother behind this?'

Every part of him railed against this intrusion into the deepest part of his psyche. 'How could you know that?'

'Because I can't think of anything more terrible than betrayal by a mother, and whatever wounded you to this extent has to be that bad.'

'You know all about me in five minutes?' he demanded scornfully.

'I knew you from the moment I met you.' She said this with blinding honesty 'From that second on, Ethan, I knew you.'

For the longest moment neither of them spoke, and then he told her some of it.

'One man did this to you, Ethan?' Savannah's face contorted with disbelief, and her eyes betrayed her bitter disappointment that Ethan didn't trust her more than that.

'I don't believe you. I can't believe this was some random attack. There isn't a man alive who could do this to you.' Her eyes narrowed in thought. 'Unless you were unconscious at the time—were you unconscious? Did someone drug you to do this?'

'It would be a cold day in hell before that happened.'

He must have been attacked by a gang, Savannah reasoned. The way Ethan had described his stepfather, the man had been a cowardly weed who wouldn't have had the strength to hold Ethan down and inflict such terrible injuries.

'Can we drop the subject?' he snapped, jolting her out of her calculations.

'No, we can't,' she said bluntly. 'I want the truth, Ethan—all of it. We just did some very adult things, and it's time you stopped treating me like a child.'

CHAPTER SIXTEEN

ETHAN'S naked torso looked as though a pitchfork with serrated edges had been dragged back and forth across it several times. 'A gang of men must have done this to you,' Savannah insisted, sure she was right now.

'You tell me,' Ethan snarled, 'Since you seem to know so much about it.'

The tension in him frightened her. Wound up so tight, he surely had to snap. But she wouldn't let it go. She couldn't let it go. If she couldn't reach out now and touch him, she never would. She went for his machismo with all guns blazing. 'If a gang of thugs attacked you it's nothing to be ashamed of.'

'*Ashamed?*' Ethan roared, exactly as she'd hoped. 'You think I'm ashamed?'

His fury filled the room, but as the window of opportunity opened she climbed through it. 'What am I supposed to think if you won't tell me?'

'May I suggest you don't think about it at all, since it's no concern of yours?'

Savannah's heart was hammering in her chest at the thought of what she'd started, but if Ethan held back now there was no hope for him—for them. 'If we mean anything to each other.' She could see the black void in Ethan, but stubbornly she kept right on blundering towards it. 'If you can't trust me.'

He was already reaching for his shirt. 'Get dressed,' he said, tossing her clothes onto the bed. He couldn't wait to leave her. She'd gone too far.

Savannah dressed quickly, determined to finish what she'd started, and with everything half-fastened and hanging off her shoulders she raced to the door. Pressing her back against it, she barred his way. 'Tell me—tell me everything, Ethan. I won't move until you do.'

He looked down at her from his great height as if she were an annoying flea he might choose to flick out of his way. She braced herself against the look in his eyes, and against the knowledge that Ethan could always use the simple expedient of lifting her out of his way. His expression assured her he had considered that, but to her immense relief he eased back. Several seconds passed while they measured each other and then he started speaking.

'A gang of men attacked me with baseball bats. When I was unconscious they cut me.' He said this with all the expression of a man reading out a shopping list. 'Are you satisfied, Savannah?'

'Not nearly.' She felt so sick she could hardly stand. 'Why did they do that?' she demanded.

'Don't push it.'

'Why?'

'I don't talk about this—not to you, not to anyone.'

He held her gaze, unblinking, until she was forced to look away.

'You were lucky to survive—'

'I said I don't talk about it.' His expression had turned to stone.

'You were lucky to retain your mobility. There must be many who have not been so fortunate.'

'Savannah,' he growled in warning.

'Or who have lived to tell the tale.'

'Comprehend this,' he snarled, bringing his face menacingly close. 'I don't want your understanding, and I sure as hell don't want your pity.' Pulling back abruptly, he unlocked the door and left the room.

She had prepared for this, but, even so, Savannah was stunned for a moment. The energy from Ethan's fury still rang in her ears, disorientating her, but she rallied quickly. Chasing after him, straightening her clothes as she ran, she followed him up the stairs. The lights had been dimmed as the staff had gone to bed, and tall, black shadows crossed with Ethan's, joining them by a tenuous thread. Driving herself to the limit, Savannah took the stairs two by two.

Catching hold of her as she came up to him on the landing, Ethan swung her round. 'Do you and I speak the same language?' he demanded, trapping her against the wall.

She fought him, warned him to get off her and railed at him, but Ethan stole each impassioned word from her lips with a kiss.

'Hiding the evidence of your arousal?' Ethan taunted, as when he released her she stood with the back of her hand across her mouth.

'I love you. Of course I respond to you. I have nothing to hide.' She pulled her hand away, revealing her love-swollen lips. 'Why do you hide your pain from me, Ethan?'

'My pain?' Ethan laughed. 'Spare me the psychobabble.'

'Is it too close to home?'

He greeted this with a contemptuous sound.

'So now you return to your ivory tower,' Savannah observed. 'And I go home?'

'It's safer for you there.'

'Safer,' Savannah repeated, shaking her head. 'There's no compromise with you, is there?'

'No,' Ethan confirmed.

'Then by those same rules you have to accept I won't give up on you.'

As the light played on Ethan's hard, set face, he folded his arms and leaned back against the door.

Ethan continued to stare at her with his dark eyes slumberous and knowing Savannah wanted him to seduce her all over again. He held a dangerous power over her, she realised, and that power was addictive. The pleasure Ethan could deliver was unimaginable, and she would never get enough of him. But with his warm, hard body possessing her, the realities of life would always be shut out. 'I won't leave until you tell me how you got those,' she said, refocusing determinedly.

He laughed. 'You're refusing to leave my house?'

'What's the worst that can happen, Ethan—you tear up my contract?' His eyes narrowed with surprise, as if that had never occurred to him. 'Your life is far more important to me than a recording contract.' The moment this was out in the open, Savannah felt naked and vulnerable. She would give up everything for Ethan, she realised, and now he knew that too. If he laughed at her now, everything was over.

Ethan remained where he was, with his arms folded, quietly watching her.

She pressed him again about his scars. 'Please,' she entreated, holding out her hands to him.

'Believe me, you don't want to know,' Ethan said, shifting position.

It was a start; it was a chink of light at the end of the tunnel and she groped towards it. 'Perhaps you think I'm too young to share this with you, though not to take to bed?' she suggested.

Ethan shrugged, and in the same monotone he'd used before he told her about the beatings that had started when he was little, and had gone on until he was too big for them, when his stepfather had employed a gang of thugs to finish the job. His stepfather's timing had been impeccable, she learned. He had chosen the week Ethan had heard he'd won a coveted place on the England rugby squad to finish the job.

'So I would never play again. And, as a bonus, he had me scarred.'

Ethan's early life had been so very different from her own, Savannah could hardly take it in. But it made everything clear, she realised as he went on. 'Before his arrest my stepfather and mother came to visit me in hospital. He must have wanted to be certain the job had been completed to his satisfaction before handing over his money, I imagine.'

Savannah's stomach churned at the thought of so much evil. 'Go on,' she prompted softly.

'His main purpose was to ensure no one would ever look at me again without revulsion, and who better to test this on than my mother?'

'I can't believe your own mother would turn from you. Surely that was the very moment when she would draw you to her heart?'

'Your experience of childhood was very different to mine. Let's just say my stepfather got his money's worth.'

'No, let's not,' Savannah argued fiercely. 'He failed. If anyone notices your scars, you make them forget. You have a bigger heart and a bigger presence than your step-father could possible imagine.'

'And there's a grisly fascination about me that makes me irresistible to the ladies?' Ethan interrupted dryly. 'Yes, I know that too.'

'Don't you dare suggest that's how I feel, because it's just not true. You're more of a man than anyone I know. And, as for your stepfather…' Savannah's rage was all the more vivid for being contained. 'The little worm!' she managed finally.

As Ethan's eyes flickered she poured her love into him. There was just a single step dividing them and she took it. Winding her arms around his neck, she stared into his eyes. 'I can't leave you like this.'

Gently untangling her arms, Ethan pulled away. 'Give up on this, Savannah.'

'Never!' But she could feel him withdrawing into himself, and she didn't know how to pull him back.

'Goodnight, Savannah.'

She heard the note of finality in his voice, and as Ethan turned away she wondered if she would ever be able to forget this moment and what might have been, or close her heart to the possibility of love.

Savannah's eyes were still drugged with sleep when her searching hands acknowledged an empty bed. Of course her bed was empty. Ethan wasn't here. Ethan never had been here in the way she'd wanted him to be, and last night he had made it clear he never would be. Fumbling for the light switch, she grimaced when she saw the time. He must have been up for hours saying goodbye to his friends, and hopefully, she wasn't too late to do the same.

When she entered the dining-room everyone cheered.

'What?' Savannah said, smiling as she stared around. Ethan's stare was boring into her, but she couldn't ignore those happy faces round the table.

Ethan's voice curled round her, underscoring her sense of loss. 'Your CD just debuted at number one on the classical charts.'

Number one? She should feel something. This was what she and the team behind her had been working towards for years. Her career was important to Ethan's record company, Savannah registered numbly, so she was pleased for him.

She had everything to be grateful for, she told herself firmly, prompting her reluctant facial muscles into a smile.

'We'll want your autograph before we leave,' one of the players teased, understandably oblivious to Savannah's troubled state of mind.

'And could you sign this for my sister?' asked another. 'My sister dreams of being a singer like you one day.'

Savannah jolted round immediately. 'I'll do better than that,' she offered. 'Piece of paper, anyone?' Ethan tore a sheet from a pad and handed it to her. Resting it on a magazine, she scribbled something and handed it to the player. 'Give this to your sister. It's my telephone number. Tell her to ring me. I'll give her any help I can.' Who knew more about dreams than she did?

Playing a role helped her get through the rest of the morning, and then the happy hostess standing at the leading man's side waved off the team.

Ethan waited until the coach was out of sight before asking Savannah to accompany him to his study.

'What's this?' Savannah said as he handed her an envelope. She gazed in dread at it, as if it contained the ashes of her future.

'It's your first-class ticket home.' His stare was unswerving, and the fact that he'd put acres of desk between them wasn't lost on her. Closing her fingers around the envelope, she wanted to say something, anything, but the words just wouldn't come.

'I didn't think you'd want to travel back with the team.' Ethan had put her welfare first again, Savannah registered dully, as if he were her business manager rather than her lover. 'And I thought you should travel home in style.' He said this as if that style was the panacea for all ills.

'Travel home in style?' Savannah repeated.

'My chauffeur will take you to the airport, and from there you'll—'

'Ethan,' she cut across him. 'I don't need a chauffeur to take me to the airport, and I don't need to travel home in style.'

'There's around an hour until you leave.' He might not have heard her. 'It shouldn't take you long to pack, should it?'

Some toiletries and two evening gowns? 'No, it shouldn't take long.'

'Good. That's settled, then. And I don't want you worrying about the paparazzi.'

Ethan was nothing if not efficient, Savannah thought, already anticipating his next reassurances concerning security, guards and alarms.

'So you'll be fine,' he finished.

If that was all it took, Savannah thought wistfully, expressing her thanks. Learning what she had about him, she could understand why Ethan's heart had grown so cold, but not why he refused to embrace the chance of love.

'Okay?' he said with one of those brief, forced smiles people used to bring an encounter to an end.

'Okay,' she agreed with the same false gusto.

Ethan had his fists planted on the desk and was leaning towards her, as if keen to underline his concern. Savannah thought she knew why. She was the valuable property of Ethan's record company, and it made sense to protect her. This was no personal relationship, other than in her self-deluded head. She stuck the envelope in the back pocket of her jeans, and when Ethan looked as if he was waiting for her to say something more she managed, 'First class? Exciting.'

'My apologies. I couldn't free up the jet for you, because I need to use it.'

'No problem,' she assured him. If Ethan wasn't with her who cared where she sat? But…more leg-room with the heart ache? She'd take it. 'I'll get ready, then.'

What more was there to say? Should she beg Ethan to let her stay on? And, if he agreed, could she ever soften him?

The reality of a man who had proved to be absolutely untouchable chilled her to the core. It was better to leave now before she said or did something she'd regret, Savannah concluded. She loved Ethan with all her heart, but in his eyes she could see not even a flicker of encouragement. Having thanked him again for the arrangements he'd so kindly made for her, she did the only thing possible and left.

CHAPTER SEVENTEEN

HE LISTENED to the limousine crunch across the gravel as it carried Savannah to the airport, waiting for the rush of relief that never came. She had sought him out immediately before leaving to thank him for his *hospitality*. His hospitality? When she'd left him to go and pack, he'd sat brooding in his study, supposedly finalising a bid for a country home in Surrey, but his thoughts were all of Savannah. He wouldn't inflict himself on her, which was the only reason he let her go. She was young and idealistic, and in time she'd come to see he was right. He was glad she had gone, he brooded, gazing out of the window at a view that was no longer perfect without Savannah in it. Perhaps if he repeated that mantra long enough he would come to believe it.

He pictured her face and remembered her parting words: 'You have a beautiful home, Ethan; take care of it. And start painting again.' She had smiled hopefully at him as she'd said this, adding, 'You have a real talent.'

For the macabre?

'Yours is the talent,' he'd told her.

'Paint some happy scenes, Ethan, and don't hide them away—put them on display.'

It was shorthand they both understood for 'keep the lights on'.

Savannah had done more than bring the *palazzo* to life, she had held up a mirror to his life, giving him a tantalising glimpse of how it could be. Which was all the more reason to set that pure heart free. He wouldn't weigh Savannah down with his dark legacy. Savannah deserved better than that, better than him, and with her career going from strength to strength there was no reason why she couldn't have it.

It was like the bottom falling out of your world twice, Savannah concluded as she closed the front door on the bailiffs. She was still reeling from her parting from Ethan, and had barely been back at the farmhouse in England five minutes when the two men had knocked at the door.

It was like a black-comedy sketch, she decided, crossing the room to put the kettle on the Aga; a very black comedy-sketch.

'Your parents have taken on too much credit, love,' the bailiffs had told her when she had assured them with matching determination that they must have got the wrong address. Unfortunately, the two men had had the right address and there was no mistake. They had shown her the legal documents they'd brought with them, and she had checked out the court order line by hateful line. The only reason they'd cut her a bit of slack was because they had wanted her autograph.

Understanding they were only doing their job, she had given them that before going to the bank to take out enough cash to send them away happy.

As she nursed her mug of tea, Savannah could only be thankful she hadn't got round to spending a penny of the money from her first royalty-cheque before she'd left for Rome. At least she had been able to put that money to good use now. But how could this have happened? She had asked herself this same question over and over again. How could her parents' world fall apart like this in the space of a few days?

But it wasn't a few days, Savannah reflected, walking to the window and staring out bleakly at the well-kept yard. It was years of paying for the best teachers, the best gowns, and even the lovingly polished second-hand grand piano in the dining-room. It was years of sacrifice for her. And she hadn't seen it before. She had grown up taking such things for granted—the golf club, the tennis club, all the right places and all the right clothes—and all these things cost more money than her parents had, or could make from the farm.

'We've seen it all before,' one of the bailiffs had assured her as he'd taken an inventory of her parents' possessions. 'And not just in the leafy lanes where the people with money live, but more and more frequently on working farms just like this one.' He'd paused then and looked at her as if even he, collecting money from hard-stretched individuals for a living, had never quite got over the calamity that had hit the farming community.

Foot-and-mouth, Savannah reflected bleakly. The disease had devastated the countryside and the people that lived there, killing their cattle, killing their dreams. So many farmers had been forced to adapt or go under. Blinking away her melancholy, she forced her mind round to practical issues.

The court order still stood, and it was up to her to get this mess sorted out before her parents returned from their cruise. Returning to the kitchen table, she sat down to make a list. But as she stared at the page of jottings in front of her she realised she could only raise half the money needed. And if she didn't come up with a solution by the end of the month the bank would foreclose and there'd be no farm. Heartache reminded her of Ethan. Briefly she considered asking him for a loan, but quickly discounted it because he would never let her pay him back. He might have the riches of Croesus, but that money wasn't hers to dip into. No. She would find her own solution.

An unexpected phone call provided Savannah with an equally unexpected opportunity, but not one she could take up. 'I'm the last person on earth who has any influence over Ethan Alexander,' she explained to the senior official from the Rugby Football Union. But the man from the governing body of English rugby was persistent, and as he went on talking Savannah thought she saw an opportunity that might just turn out to be the saving of them all.

'And I said no!' Frowning, Ethan sprang up from his swivel chair and began to pace the long-suffering floor of his study. 'My rugby days are over. You know that,' he snapped at the official from the RFU. 'Yes, what I'm saying is your suggestion is out of bounds. I can't possibly make it fly for you—and no is my final answer.

'What?' Ethan ground his jaw as the man kept on talking. 'No, I didn't know that—when did this happen?' His expression turned grim as he listened to the official's account of a recent news item he'd missed due to a business trip. He might say no to a lot of things, but he would never turn his back on Savannah.

'No' could no longer be his final answer.

* * *

Almost exactly a month later Savannah stood on a newly levelled field at her parents' farm, waiting for Ethan's helicopter to arrive. She had anticipated this moment, spending many sleepless nights planning for it—planning that had included closing off part of her heart that would never be brought into service again.

Everyone had rejoiced on the day Ethan had agreed to be patron of the rugby academy set on her parents' farm. Savannah had quietly celebrated, knowing it marked his return to the world. From the moment Ethan had given his agreement, things had moved quickly. Savannah had persuaded her parents to enter into a long-term lease with the RFU for the use of some land, and that money had saved the farm. She couldn't have felt more passionate about this opening today for all sorts of reasons, and the only anxiety she had was seeing Ethan again. As Ethan's helicopter cast a shadow over the field, she told herself she could handle it, and what better time than this? Everything was in place, and even the local mayor had accepted her invitation to cut the ribbon outside the new clubhouse. But seeing his face at the controls undid all her good intentions. Ethan helped so many people, and yet the one person Ethan seemed incapable of helping was himself. This would be their first face-to-face meeting since they parted in Tuscany, and she loved him as much as ever. But this was no time to be nursing a broken heart. The project was far too important for that. And now she must greet the guest of honour.

He saw her immediately. Even amongst the crowd of excited children and local dignitaries, she stood out. Savannah had real presence, and the place she still held in his heart drew him to her.

Though she should be in Salzburg giving a recital today, he remembered, not standing on a rugby pitch dressed in a track-suit and trainers with her hair drawn back in a simple ponytail but never looking more beautiful. Right now she was running on the spot, surrounded by a group of youngsters, as if sport was her only passion now.

He was hugely disappointed, but the love he felt for Savannah would never change. He had come because he would do anything on earth to help Savannah and her family, and this scheme she'd dreamed up benefited everybody. Which was so like her. Savannah Ross might be the most irritating woman he had ever met, but Savannah always put others before herself.

The next few hours were going to be tough training for a life without Savannah, but where that was concerned he hadn't changed his mind. He was still scarred and she was still beautiful—inside and out. Some things never changed.

As he ducked his head to clear the rotor blades he caught a glimpse of her pale face angled towards him at the edge of the field. Was she smiling? He hoped not. He hoped she would only remember the distance he had put between them before she'd left Tuscany. He didn't want to see a look of love in her eyes. He wanted to know she had moved on.

They would never have worked as a couple, he told himself firmly as he strode towards her. How could he live with someone with no sense of responsibility? Though the fact that Savannah had broken her contractual obligations had surprised him. This youth project was vital, but she didn't need to be here. She had sacrificed a great career move, and in doing so had put herself at risk of having her contract terminated.

Now he was within touching distance, he registered

explosions of sensation. He didn't trust himself to shake her hand, and was glad when the current manager of the England squad intervened. He moved on with relief, spearheading the group responsible for making this day a reality, conscious that Savannah was behind him. *As beautiful as ever, with her skin as flawless as porcelain, and her eyes...*

He breathed a sigh of relief as he approached the line of local dignitaries, but as he fell into easy conversation he was conscious of Savannah's wildflower scent coupled with her breathy laugh. But she'd let his team down, he reminded himself grimly, and anyone who did that let him down. As she'd shunned her engagement to sing in Salzburg to be here, Ethan was under pressure from his team to end her contract.

His heart lifted when he met the first youngster on the scheme, and he recognised the same determination to succeed he'd had blazing from the boy's eyes. It was more than possible that one of these boys would play for England some day, and he knew then that that even without Savannah's involvement this was the type of project he would gladly give his last penny to.

'But this time your money isn't enough,' one of the officials told Ethan goodnaturedly, glancing at Savannah, who had joined their little group for confirmation of this.

He didn't need his attention being drawn to Savannah when he was conscious of her every second. His attention might appear to be focused on the RFU official, but he was communing with her on some other level. His feelings towards her were as turbulent as ever, but he could understand now why she was so reluctant to leave the countryside for the anonymous bustle of the opera world. However prestigious that world might be, it lacked the honest goodness of the soil, and the unspoiled beauty of these rolling fields and ancient trees. The delicate tracery of lush, green hedges and dry stone-walls surrounding her parents' farm created a quintessentially English scene, and one which he was even buying into with his purchase of the adjoining land. But even as a result of everything he could see here Savannah shouldn't have broken her agreement and let people down.

He was snapped out of these thoughts by officials ushering him into the recently erected club-house for tea. As he turned he found Savannah at his side. He steeled himself. What he had to say to her wouldn't be easy, and so he greeted her formally before glancing towards the private office where they wouldn't be overheard. 'Could I have a moment of your time?'

'Hello, Ethan,' she said softly, reminding him of another occasion when his fast-ticking clock had ruled out the space for proper introductions. He felt a pang of remorse for then, for now, for everything that could never be. And what was he thinking? Was he going to take her aside and tell her she'd lost her contract on this wonderful occasion for which she was largely responsible? Was that his way now? The look in Savannah's eyes contained a disturbing degree of understanding. She knew him too well. She knew that once his mind was made up there could be no turning back, but as she turned to walk ahead of him he did wonder at the flicker of steel in her gaze.

He launched in without preamble, listing all the reasons why breaking her contract to attend the opening of a training facility that had nothing to do with her career was unacceptable. She stared at him throughout with little reaction other than a paling of her lips. He always gave right of reply in these circumstances, and when she didn't speak up immediately he prompted her.

He was shocked by the way Savannah's face contorted with fury, and then she croaked something unintelligible at him. 'If you'd just calm down,' he said with dignity, 'Perhaps I'd be able to understand what it is you're trying to say.'

She made a gesture, like a cutting motion across her throat.

'That's a bit over-dramatic, isn't it?' he commented with a humourless laugh.

'I've lost my voice,' she half-huffed, half-squeaked at him.

Every swear-word in the book flew through his head then. He'd been so wound up like a spring at the thought of seeing her again, he hadn't even paused to consider all the facts. So a sore throat accounted for her no-show in Salzburg.

'Please forgive me,' he said stiffly. He couldn't blame her for the way she was looking at him. He never made mistakes, and therefore lacked the technique to account for them. Or maybe he did make mistakes—maybe he had—and maybe the biggest mistake of all was his under-estimating Savannah. She was an integral part of this training project. He'd learned from the officials at the RFU that this training facility was all Savannah's idea, and that she had come up with the plan of leasing part of her parents' land to the club so they could have a proper training-facility for the youth squad, as well as all the other local youngsters who wanted to come along and taste the sport. There were scholarships and training programmes and grading examinations the various groups could work towards—funded by him, but all of it dreamed up by Savannah.

More silent swear-words accompanied this thought, with the addition of a grimace and a self-condemning shake of the head. 'Savannah, please accept my apologies, I didn't realise…'

If he had expected benediction and forgiveness, he was out of luck. Spearing him a look, she spun on her heels and left him flat.

CHAPTER EIGHTEEN

HE FOUND her in the cosy farmhouse kitchen where she was standing by the Aga, drinking a steaming glass full of something aromatic. She barely looked up when he walked in, and, other than stirring her brew thoughtfully with a stumpy cinnamon-stick, she didn't move. 'Savannah.'

Her eyes were wounded and her mouth was both trembling and determined when she did turn to look at him. She gestured for him to stay away from her, but since when had he ever taken orders? He stopped short halfway across the kitchen when he saw the tears in her eyes, and his guts twisted at the thought of what he'd done. 'Savannah, please.'

She shook her head and gestured that he should stay away from her.

'I had no idea. I just got back—I came straight here.'

She shrugged her shoulders, and made a sound that showed more clearly than words that she couldn't give a fig what he did, and her blue eyes had turned to stone.

'I should have double checked my facts before wading in, but I just wanted to…'

Her finely etched brows rose in ironic question.

'All right, then,' he admitted, raking his hair with stiff, angry fingers. 'I just wanted to see you. There, I've said it.'

She huffed.

'Savannah, please.'

Lifting her tiny hand, she used it to push him away.

He wasn't as easy as that to get rid of.

How was she supposed to have a go at him when she couldn't even speak? Gestures and angry looks only got you so far—and that wasn't nearly far enough where Ethan was concerned. 'You can't just walk in here and act like nothing happened.' She wasn't sure how much of that Ethan got, seeing as she could barely force a sound that wasn't a squeak out of her infected throat.

'You should be out there, enjoying your success,' he said, confirming her impression that he hadn't understood a word of what she'd said. She pulled a face. What was the point going outside without Ethan? The scheme needed him—and not just to give it a popular face. She needed him to take on a fuller role than that, but right now her angry look was telling him: *you're a selfish, egocentric brute, Ethan Alexander, and I never want to see you again.*

But Ethan remained undeterred. 'So, just as a matter of interest, who is taking your place in Salzburg?'

'Madame de Silva,' she managed to husk.

He smiled, remembering Savannah had looked sensational in Madame de Silva's slinky gown, which was another reason he'd been only too eager to drag her off the pitch. But while he was reminiscing the wounded look returned to Savannah's eyes. 'But Madame couldn't look half as beautiful as you do right now in your track-suit,' he assured her gently.

And before he could stop himself he dipped his head

and kissed her very gently on the lips. He thought for a horrible moment she was going to push him away. She was certainly crying again; he could feel her tears wetting his face, and he could taste them.

'You'll catch it,' she warned, her eyes wide with concern when he released her.

'Your sore throat, do you mean? I certainly hope so,' he said, kissing her again.

She wasn't nearly finished with saying hello to Ethan yet, as he released her when the door opened and everyone piled in. In typical English spring fashion the rain had chosen that moment to pour down, and there wasn't enough space in the club house or even the large marquee her parents had erected to accommodate everyone who had turned up for the opening ceremony.

Ethan quickly went about introducing himself to her parents, and then Savannah watched him mingling easily with everyone else. They had a marvellous team of workers on the farm, some of whose families had lived on the land adjoining theirs for generations. It was thanks to these lifelong friends that Savannah's parents had been in a position to accept Ethan's offer of a cruise, and she was glad he had the opportunity to meet them and thank them personally. Maybe Ethan could never be part of her life, but perhaps he understood now how special her life on the farm was, and how family and friends were a precious and integral part of that life.

As Savannah watched Ethan ease his powerful frame through the crowd of noisy visitors in the cosy farmhouse kitchen, it wasn't possible to think of him as the same man she'd first met. When he came out to socialise he radiated friendliness. Perhaps that should be her next project. If she could bring youngsters with similar injuries to

Ethan's into contact with him, he could give them the confidence to live their lives to the fullest.

Was she only dreaming, or would that really be possible? The first step would be persuading Ethan to take a full part in the scheme…

She would just have to try a little harder, Savannah concluded, passing round the savouries she'd baked. 'Ethan.' She caught up with him by the window, where he was holding a conversation with the local mayor. It was so hard to make him hear her with a scratchy voice. 'Excuse me,' she squeaked politely. 'Do you think I could borrow you for a moment?'

'Would you excuse me?' Ethan asked the mayor politely.

As soon as they found a space, she launched right in, 'Ethan, we need you.'

'You're speaking again?' His facial expression ran the gamut from relief to wry to mock-weary in the space of a breath.

'Happily, my voice is coming back,' Savannah agreed, ignoring Ethan's groan. She couldn't sing the praises of hot water, honey and lemon stirred with a cinnamon stick highly enough.

'Sorry?' Ethan dipped his head very low until his ear was level with her mouth. 'You'll have to speak up; you're still croaking,' he teased, turning Savannah's ailment to his advantage.

'If you think you're going to distract me with that wicked look…' He probably would, she realised.

'Go on,' Ethan prompted.

'We need you, Ethan,' she said, not messing about. 'And not just for a flying visit every now and then.'

'Ah…' He looked down at her sternly, but he was smiling inwardly as he remembered the house he'd bought close by. He'd see Savannah, though what she was proposing for the scheme was a step too far for him. He couldn't let the youngsters see his scars and put them off their game. 'You've touched on the one subject I'm not prepared to discuss,' he said flatly, and when she squeaked at him he put up his hand. 'Are you quite sure your throat is getting better? Only I can't tell you how peaceful it's been since you lost your voice.'

'Well, I found it,' Savannah assured him firmly. 'And it's getting better all the time.'

'No,' Ethan said flatly when Savannah put her proposition to him outside the club house by the fence. 'How many times do I have to say no to this idea of yours?'

'As many times as you're asked—until you say yes,' she told him steadily.

'Savannah, I should warn you, I don't succumb to pressure.'

'There has been the odd occasion,' she reminded him brazenly, using tactics she should be thoroughly ashamed of but wasn't.

'Don't you know you're playing with fire?' he warned, seeing her eyes darken.

'Am I?' she asked. She was all innocence as she angled her face towards him. 'Perhaps that's because I'll stop at nothing to get you properly into this scheme.'

'Well, I never thought you'd sink this low,' Ethan murmured with his lips very close to her mouth.

'Then you have a great deal to learn about me.'

Dragging her close, he kissed her again.

'Though I have to admit,' she admitted breathlessly when Ethan released her, 'That I usually try to make sure that when you and fire are concerned there's no one else around.'

Breaking off to say hello to some of the England squad—who, dressed in kit, were leading a group of youngsters out onto the pitch—he couldn't have agreed more. The moment he turned back to her, she said, 'I won't give up, you know.'

'I think I guessed that much,' he told her, drawing her after him.

'Where are you taking me?'

'Somewhere we can talk privately and your enthusiasm can be harnessed.'

'Sounds lovely,' she murmured as he helped her over a stile.

'It will be.' Vaulting over the same stile, he took her by the hand and led her waist-deep through a field of long grass.

'Well, I think we can talk here,' she agreed when he finally stopped in the middle of it.

'You can talk if you want to.'

'Ethan…'

Love, contentment and unimaginable happiness…as well as a nice, dewy meadow freshly watered by the rain. 'Thank goodness, you're underneath me,' Savannah murmured groggily to Ethan some time later.

'I didn't want you getting grass stains on your nice, new track-suit,' Ethan mocked softly as they recovered.

'Why worry? The sun is shining now and I'll soon dry out.' As she outlined Ethan's sensual mouth with her fingertip until he threatened to bite it off, Savannah wondered whether this was the right time to broach the subject at the forefront of her mind or not.

'Well?' Ethan pressed, knowing she had something on her mind.

'Well, what?' she said, pulling on her innocent face. 'Why must you always be so suspicious of me?'

'I might only have known you a short time, but I know there's usually something brewing when you have that look.'

She hesitated and then said bluntly, 'When you sprang over that stile…'

'Yes?' He wasn't going to help her.

'Well, I just thought, with your back and—'

'Oh, I see.' Moving his head, he dislodged her teasing finger. 'You want to know how I can do something like that when I can't play rugby. Or, more importantly—at least as far as your scheme is concerned—why I won't help out with the coaching.'

'Yes,' Savannah admitted, wriggling away from him and sitting up. Truthfully, she had a lot more in mind for Ethan than the occasional coaching session. She wanted him to take a much fuller role in the scheme for which he had already proved to be an inspirational figurehead.

'It's only weights landing on my back I have to be careful about,' he explained. 'My legs are fine.'

'Then…' Hugging her knees, she rested her chin on them, staring up at him.

'Then?'

'Stop pretending you don't know what I mean. And stop growling at me,' she added when Ethan made a mock-threatening sound. She fixed a stare on him. 'If there's nothing wrong with your legs, there can't be any reason why you can't take part in the training pro-gramme—just part-time, of course,' she added before Ethan could get a word in. 'Plus, the occasional guest ap-pearance would make all the difference.'

Having buckled his belt, Ethan sat up beside her and

swung Savannah onto his knee. 'Is that what all this has been leading up to?'

'Not all of it,' she admitted truthfully.

'Well, at least you've got the decency to blush,' he observed dryly, drawing her into his shoulder.

'You still haven't given me your answer, Ethan.'

'Well, why don't I do that now?'

It was some time later when Ethan drew Savannah to her feet. As he helped to brush grass and twigs from her clothes, she sensed something had changed.

'My answer is no,' he told her quietly, confirming her worst fears. 'How can I let those kids see my scars? They'll see nothing else—they won't concentrate on the game, on my coaching—I'd hold them back.'

'No, you wouldn't.'

'For the last time, Savannah, no coaching sessions.'

Seizing his hands, she stared into his eyes. 'What if we brought other youngsters here—youngsters with disfigurements like yours—would you do it then? Would you bring everyone together so that no one was an outsider?'

She had silenced him and touched him as only Savannah could. 'I'll think about it,' he promised, silencing her in the most effective way he could. 'Now, will you be quiet?' he demanded when he released her.

'Of course I will,' Savannah agreed, tipping her chin to stare lovingly at him. 'The moment you agree.'

CHAPTER NINETEEN

THE REST of the day passed in whirl of activity, with Savannah and Ethan falling naturally into the role of host and hostess. They were a good team, Savannah thought, smiling across the crowded club-house at Ethan. No, she'd got that wrong—they were an excellent team—but she must stop looking at him as if she had to convince herself he was really there. She was feeling more confident he would agree to a little coaching. Hadn't he said as much when they were making love in the meadow? Or was it coaching her he'd had in mind? Time to pin him down, she decided as people started to drift off home.

When Ethan came to her he raised both her hands to his lips. Had the tender lover returned to her? She had to believe that was so. Conscious of her mother and father watching them from the other side of the room, she sighed with pleasure as Ethan brushed her cheeks with his lips.

'It's been a wonderful day, Savannah,' he told her gently. 'Thank you so much…'

'It's nothing,' she murmured. She was still staring up at him, feeling like she could fly.

'I want to thank you on behalf of everyone,' he added,

still holding her hands in his firm grip. 'And I promise to give serious thought to your suggestion.'

But? She could hear a 'but'. 'Thank you, Ethan.' Savannah's smile faded. There was something wrong. She could see no answering warmth in Ethan's eyes, just a rather detached interest. 'You're not going to take an active part, are you?'

'I'm the patron, and I've already donated a large amount of money.'

'I'm not talking about money, Ethan, the scheme needs you—hands-on you.' There was something else, Savannah suspected—something Ethan hadn't told her.

He released her hands. 'Anything else at all, you only have to ask.'

'I am asking. If everyone else can find time, why can't you?'

'You know why,' Ethan said grimly.

No, she didn't—and now he was being drawn away. She'd monopolised him too long, and all the people who had been waiting to say goodbye to him were jostling for his attention. She waited on tenterhooks until he was free again and then pounced. 'Ethan, look at me.' But there were more interruptions. How hard was it to do this in public when you were trying to capture the attention of the most important man in the room?

Ethan freed himself this next time. He'd seen her concern and he crossed the room to her side. 'Tell me,' he said.

'Everyone needs your magic,' she said. 'Just look around you…' There was a group of youngsters clustered round the team captain. They might be with one hero, but they were all looking at Ethan, the most formidable man in the room, with awe-struck stares. 'They need you. Just a few hours of your time, Ethan. They rate you so highly.'

'You know my position.'

'No, I don't!' Savannah exclaimed. 'Your scars? They know about your scars—they don't even notice them. What else is holding you back?'

Ethan's eyes narrowed. 'What makes you think there's anything else?'

'I know you, Ethan.'

'Enough,' he said sharply, leaning close. Putting his arm out, Ethan rested his clenched fist against the wall so that Savannah's face and his were shielded from the crowd. 'I'll do anything I can for these young people.'

'Then give them your time. Or can't you bear the thought of being on the same pitch as a bunch of enthusiastic amateurs? Aren't they good enough for you, Ethan?'

He knew she was goading him, reaching deep, and that she didn't believe it for one moment. 'Savannah,' he warned, his mouth almost brushing her lips now.

'No, I won't be quiet,' she replied, confirming his thoughts. 'You're due a wake-up call.'

'And who better to give it to me than you?' He didn't wait for her answer. Freeing the latch on the door behind her, he backed her through it holding on to her while he closed the door behind them, and then frogmarched her across the yard.

And still she peppered him with accusations. 'You paint wonderful pictures and hide them away—that's one precious gift wasted. You're an inspiration, a positive role-model for young people and a force for good—a second—'

Savannah gasped as Ethan thrust her through the entrance of the hay barn. Slamming the door shut, he shot the bolt. 'This time I talk and you listen,' he said. Bringing her in front of him, he held her firmly in place.

'I live my life causing the least inconvenience I can to everyone around me.'

'You mean you're stuck in the past and won't even glance into the future?'

'I'm sure my business analysts might have something to say about that,' he said with all the confidence of a hugely successful tycoon.

'Your business analysts? And I bet they keep you warm at night.'

'You don't know me, so just leave this—'

'I know enough about you to care.'

As her voice echoed in the lofty barn they both went still. Ethan's eyes were so dark and reflected a truth so terrible Savannah almost wished she hadn't brought him to this point. 'What is it, Ethan?' she said, reaching out to touch his face. 'Who did this terrible thing to you?' They both knew she wasn't talking about his scars.

Ethan moved his head away.

'And this time tell me,' Savannah insisted gently. 'Don't insult me with some pallid version of the truth because you've decided I can't take the facts. I can take anything for you—share everything with you—good and bad.'

Everything hung on this moment, Savannah realised, and yet all she could do now was wait.

After the longest moment, Ethan shrugged. 'My stepfather beat me.'

She knew that.

'When I grew too big for him to beat me, he paid others to do it for him.'

She knew that too. 'Go on,' she prompted softly.

'There is no more to tell.'

No more Ethan wanted to tell, perhaps. 'I don't believe

you.' Her voice barely made it above a whisper, but he'd heard her.

Ethan stared over her head as the seconds ticked past, and then he revealed his innermost demon. 'When I had recovered from the accident I visited my mother to try to heal things between us. Whatever had happened in the past, she was still my mother, and I had to believe she didn't really understand what had been going on.'

As Ethan stopped speaking Savannah felt the pain of his disappointment so keenly she didn't even need to hear the rest, but she knew she had to let him say it.

'She had known,' he said in a voice pitched low. 'My mother had known all along. She knew all of it.'

What hurt Savannah the most was that she could still hear the surprise in Ethan's voice. For a moment she found it impossible to speak or even breathe, and could only communicate the compassion she felt for him with her eyes.

'She told me I got in the way... She said I was always in the way, and that she wished I had never been born. She said she never wanted to see me again, which I could understand, really.'

'No!' As Ethan made a dismissive gesture, Savannah caught hold of his hand and held it firmly. 'No, Ethan, no; that's not right. You must never think that. You did nothing wrong—not then, not as a child, not ever.' She understood now why Ethan kept so much hidden. Having been betrayed by his own mother, how could he ever reveal his feelings to anyone again? He had to know she was here for him on any terms, Savannah determined, and that part of the bargain said she would be strong—even strong enough to let him go, if that was what Ethan really wanted.

But as he shifted position, and she saw his wounded

face set in that distant mask, she knew she had to give their chance to be together one more try.

'What better scheme than ours to bury those demons in your past once and for all? What greater triumph could you have, Ethan?'

Ethan remained silent for the longest moment, and then he murmured with a flicker of the old humour, '*Our* scheme?'

'Why not *our* scheme?'

'Because you seem to be doing pretty well on your own.'

'But we can do so much more together.' She waited for his answer, tense in every fibre of her being.

'Is that right?' he said dryly, flicking a glance her way.

At least they'd made contact, Savannah thought with relief. 'I'm sure of it,' she said fiercely.

'So you've found a way out of the darkness?'

The glint was back in Ethan's eyes—and that was more than a relief, it was a reminder of their first night together at the *palazzo*. He had come back to her. Seizing his hands, she brought them to her lips. 'We'll get through this,' she promised him.

'I already have.'

'Then you have no excuse.'

'Not to shine a light?' As Savannah smiled, he wondered how he could ever have been foolish enough to imagine life without her.

'I need you, Ethan,' she told him passionately. 'We all need you.'

'Well, I don't know about everyone,' he admitted gruffly. 'But you've got me, Ms Ross—and for keeps.'

'What are you saying, Ethan?'

'I'm saying that I love you, and that I want to be with you always.'

Savannah swallowed deep as Ethan looked at her. 'I take it you'll be staying on, then?'

'Even a rugby match couldn't keep me away from you,' Ethan assured her. 'Unless England was playing, of course…'

EPILOGUE

THE SUN blazed down from a clear, blue Tuscan sky, and there were no shadows on the day that Savannah married Ethan. The world's press had gathered in the exquisite ancient city of Florence for what everyone was calling the celebrity marriage of the year.

For the farm girl, and the tycoon better known to the world as the Bear, this was quite an occasion, Savannah thought. As the bells rang out and the crowd cheered, it was a struggle to wrap her mind around the fact that she really was married to the man she adored. Standing on time worn steps next to Ethan outside the Basilica de Santa Maria di Fiore, a cathedral church only exceeded in size by St Peter's in Rome, she only had to see the guard of honour formed by the youngsters Ethan now made time to coach on a regular basis to know that miracles did happen—and that, yes, dreams did come true.

'All right?' Ethan murmured, squeezing her arm.

Better than all right. She adored him. He was without question the most wonderful man in the world. And apart from making her so happy he had extended the reach of the training scheme—which had meant leasing more space from her parents in order to house the office of the newly expanded training business, saving the farm, as well as giving them the little luxuries they'd lived so long without.

And her recording career? Well, she'd just signed a contract to complete a new album, and after that studio work and the occasional personal appearance at the world-famous opera house Glynebourne in Lewes, Sussex, just down the road from Ethan's new home that adjoined her parents' farm. He'd told Savannah she was to have her cake and—for the sake of the large family they planned to have—to eat it as well. Their mission, the newly married couple had decided, was to fill all of Ethan's homes with love, laughter and lots of light—and if possible with a rugby team of their own.

'You look so beautiful,' Ethan said, standing a little behind Savannah so the crowd had a good view of her.

'And you are the most beautiful man on earth.' To her he was and always would be. Now Ethan's inners scars were healed, he had no blemishes. 'And I love you,' she said.

'More than life itself,' Ethan agreed, smiling into Savannah's eyes. 'Now, let them have a good look at your dress.'

Oh, yes, her dress… Her very special dress in ivory silk, lavishly embroidered with seed pearls and thousands of twinkles that sparkled in the sun. It had been lovingly made for Savannah by her regular team of seamstresses in the far north of England, who knew a thing or two about showing off the fuller figure to best advantage. Who else would she have chosen to make her wedding gown, to ensure there wasn't the slightest chance she would suffer a wardrobe malfunction similar to the one that had brought the crowd at the Stadio Flaminio to its feet in Rome? In this dress her assets were displayed to full advantage, a fact that had not gone overlooked by her adoring Bear.

'Cover yourself, woman,' Ethan growled as Savannah's silk-chiffon veil billowed back and away from her naked shoulders.

'If I don't, will you carry me off and keep me safe as you did on the day we first met?' Savannah asked him.

She managed a solemn face for as long as it took her to ask Ethan that question, and as his mouth tugged at one corner he allowed, 'With one small change.'

'Which is?'

'I wouldn't waste so much time before taking you to bed.'

'Is that a promise, husband?'

'You can count on it, wife,' he murmured as they posed for pictures.

'Then I may just have to stage-manage a wardrobe malfunction.'

'And I might just have to put you over my knee, and—'

Ethan paused, seeing the official photographer was hopping from foot to foot.

'Smile, please,' the man begged, indicating that a formal pose, rather than a lover's confab was called for.

He barely had to ask.

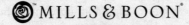
MILLS & BOON®

and

ENGLAND
RUGBY

present

INTERNATIONAL
BILLIONAIRES

*From rich tycoons to royal playboys –
they're red-hot and ruthless*

Turn the page for more!

Read all about the players, the glamour,
the excitement of the game – and where to
escape when you want some romance!

A GIRL'S GUIDE TO RUGBY

Rugby isn't just thirty sweaty men getting muddy in a field for eighty minutes – although that can be quite appealing! It's played in more than a hundred countries across five continents, by all ages and sexes. It's a fun, fast and furious spectator sport – and it's also a great family day out.

International locations
Want some winter sun? Jet off to **Dubai** for the International Rugby Sevens. Or pop to **Argentina** for a spot of tango, polo *and* rugby. Or how about a trip to **Sydney** for the **Tri Nations**?

Glamorous audience
Don't forget to keep an eye out for celebrities watching the game with you! You might spot **Prince William** and **Prince Harry** at Twickenham, or **Charlotte Church** cheering for Gavin Henson at the Millennium Stadium in Cardiff. **Zara Phillips** is also dating a rugby player.

Not just for the boys
Who knows? You may be inspired to have a go yourself! Rugby is one of the best all-round **workouts**, building strength, cardiovascular fitness and toning those all-important wobbly bits. And nothing is better than being part of a winning team!

ENGLAND
RUGBY

RUGBY – THE BASICS

First time at a match? Always wondered what a line-out was? Confused by an offside call? These basic facts will get you through!

1. **Vital statistics**
   There are fifteen players on each side. Each match lasts for eighty minutes, and the team plays forty minutes in one direction and then they swap ends.

2. **Scoring**
   The object is to score more points than the opposition. Teams can score a try, penalty, drop goal or conversion.

3. **Try**
   When the ball is grounded over the try line and within the area before the dead ball line it earns five points.

4. **Conversion**
   After a team scores a try, a conversion, a free kick at goal from a point directly in line with where the try was scored, is worth two points.

5. **Drop goal**
   When, in open play, the ball is kicked between the rugby post uprights and above the crossbar, in a drop goal, it earns three points.

6. **Penalty**
   This can be awarded by the referee for infringements of the rules of rugby and if successfully kicked it earns three points.

7. **Offside**
   This is the key rule of rugby, and it's a lot simpler than football. Say your friend has the ball and she passes it to you. If she has to throw

it *back* to you, you are onside. If she throws it *forward*, you are offside. Players must be behind the ball.

8. **Tackle**
   Not as rude as it sounds! The player with the ball is brought to the ground by a tackle, and they must either pass or release the ball.

9. **Ruck**
   If a player loses possession of the ball, the team form a ruck to try to win the ball back, trying to ruck the ball back with their feet.

10. **Maul**
    If a ball carrier is held up (a tackle which doesn't bring the player to the ground) a maul may form, when players can only join the maul from behind their team-mates and not come in from the side.

11. **Line-out**
    If the ball goes out of the field of play, into touch, a line-out restarts the game. Players from both teams form parallel lines while the ball is thrown down the middle of the line-out from the touch line and players are lifted by their team-mates in an effort to win the ball.

12. **Scrum**
    If a player infringes the rules, for example by being offside, a scrum may be awarded, where the eight forwards from each team bind together and push against the opposition to win the ball, which is fed in down the centre of the tunnel.

HOW TO BE FABULOUS
AT THE RUGBY...

Follow our simple guide to rugby style and you'll soon have a whole new perspective on the game.

- The atmosphere before any big game is part of the fun. Make sure you get there early. And starting the match-day party with a champagne picnic means it won't really matter if you know the rules or not!

- While you want to look gorgeous, you also want to be warm. Invest in a striking full-length coat and matching scarf and gloves.

- It's chilly in the stands and the weather can never be trusted – make sure your make-up is weatherproof.

- Indulge the trend for girly wellingtons or pretty ballet shoes, as sky-scraper heels may start to pinch. Especially if your team is winning and you're leaping up and down enthusiastically!

- Be ready to join in – sing as loud as you can in support of your team, cheer on the tries and allow yourself to get into the spirit of it all. You'll be surprised at how much fun you have!

- Not sure whether you'll enjoy the game? Check out Rugby Sevens. Group tournaments are played all around the UK throughout the year, and with only seven men on the pitch.

- Rugby supporters are a jolly bunch. There are many new friends to be had over a beer and a hog roast!

- A rugby game is only eighty minutes long. Why stop the afternoon there? Plan a fabulous after party and play perfect hostess.

ROMANTIC RUGBY

What better excuse than the six countries of the Six Nations to treat yourself and your partner to a romantic weekend away! You can share the fun of a match, and then enjoy a new city together.

In *The Ruthless Billionaire's Virgin*, Ethan and Savannah fall in love in one of the world's most beautiful places, Rome, the Eternal City.

Rome has scores of beautiful romantic lanes, restaurants and parks. Try escaping the crowds down the small medieval lanes leading from the busy squares – around both Campo de' Fiori and Piazza Navona there are plenty of pretty corners where you can escape the worst of the crowds. Visit some of the smaller bars and restaurants you'll find here, catering for locals as well as tourists.

During July and August parks and gardens around Rome host musical evenings catering to all tastes. Whether you'd rather listen to Verdi at the Baths of Caracalla, pop concerts on a tennis court, or free classical concerts in piazzas, Rome is packed with events every night. For an unusual and headily romantic evening in the summer months, take your beloved to the Roseto, Rome's public rose garden. In the evenings you can dine, drink, wander through the roses, enjoy views over the ruined Palatine, or enjoy food tasting and talks (in Italian).

BEHIND THE SCENES WITH THE ENGLAND TEAM

While you settle yourself in the stands and the build-up to the kick-off begins, what has been happening behind the scenes? England's Media Manager tells us:

I've been acting as England Media Manager for the senior squad for a large part of the eleven years I've spent at the Rugby Football Union. The England Media Manager job has changed a lot from the dozen or so members of the press that turned up to the first press conference I worked on in 1997 to the fifty plus we can expect in a test week and during a World Cup the numbers can exceed two hundred!!!

The rugby media are excellent, but it's always a demanding job ensuring their needs are catered for and that the media schedule complements the players' preparations for the week rather than cutting into any of their coaching and training times.

I've been fortunate enough to work on the last three RWC's, eleven RBS Six Nations Championships and over one hundred test matches, but the buzz and anticipation is always there and I enjoy every test week, either from a personal point of view or a professional one – ideally both if England win!

On the Friday before the match, the England squad train in the morning at Twickenham Stadium and the kickers practise before and after the session. The England Team Manager holds his final pre-match media session and one senior player meets the rugby writers in a huddle for ten-minute chat. Once these sessions are finished we all put the final touches together and get ready for the match itself. My department produces all the passes for the media who attend on the day, which for an England match can number over four hundred, so it's vital they all have the right passes for the game.

On the day of the game, I normally arrive at the stadium five hours before kick-off. I check the media coverage and then ensure that all the Communications team are in their respective positions around the ground. Everyone knows their role on a match day and they all do a top job. I'm always in the tunnel area to handle the media parts of England's arrival at the ground ninety minutes before kick-off, which involve a quick interview with the captain and one TV crew in the England dressing room and one TV and one radio interview with the England Team Manager pitch side.

After the game the players and England Team Manager do quick TV and radio interviews in an area we call 'the flash room' near the changing rooms. Then it's the press conference after checking with the doc first to see if there are any injuries to report. After the press conference the daily rugby writers have a chat with the England Team Manager so they have some different quotes for the Monday papers as the game is being played on a Saturday. Then the players arrive to do their interviews before they join friends and family for something to eat.

If it's a 2.30pm kick-off I'm normally home by about 8pm just in time to see the kids off to bed and then I sit down with my wife and watch a bit of TV and get some sleep before doing it all again the next week!

The atmosphere in the city was electric. Alicia Cross felt it tingle in her veins as she joined the Welsh rugby fans streaming into Cardiff's Millennium Stadium. As always they had arrived in their thousands to support their heroes, with the added excitement that today a victory against Italy would mean a step forward towards the holy grail of the Six Nations Contest, the Grand Slam of victory over all five of the other teams.

After weeks of travel and hard work to organise parties and press events, Alicia had begged a couple of hours off duty this afternoon to watch the match with friends. Earlier she had checked the arrangements for the sponsors' lunch at the stadium, then hurried back to Cardiff Bay to ensure that all was ready in the hotel chosen for the party later that night. But now at last, instead of joining the sponsors in their hospitality box, she was on her way to her seat in the stands, and she was cutting it a bit fine. In her rush almost bumped into the man who stepped in front of her, barring her way. She opened her mouth to apologise, then snapped it shut, the colour draining from her face. In a knee-jerk reaction she flung away, but he was too quick for her and seized her hand. Conscious of curious glances beamed in their direction, she forced herself to stand still, her heart thudding against her ribs as she looked up into the handsome, unforgettable face of the man who had once changed her girlhood dreams into nightmares.

"Alicia," he said, in the voice that had not, to her intense disgust, lost the power to send shivers down her spine. Eyes locked with hers, he held her hand captive.

She returned the intent, heavy-lidded gaze for the space of several, deliberate heartbeats, then wrenched her hand away and turned on her heel.

But Francesco da Luca caught her by the elbow. "Alicia, wait. I must speak with you."

She stared at him in silent disdain, refusal blazing in her eyes as a crowd of late arrivals surged through the turnstiles to jostle them, and with a smothered curse he let her go.

"Do not think you can escape me again so easily, Alicia!"

The hint of menace in the deep, husky voice sent her racing up after the other fans as though the devil were after her. She shot into the cauldron of noise and music in the famous arena, and dived down the steep steps at such breakneck speed Gareth Davies leapt up from the end of a row to seize her by the arm.

"Steady on, you'll break your neck."

"Where have you *been*?" demanded Meg

indignantly, as her brother thrust Alicia into the seat between them.

Alicia's reply was drowned by the roar from the Italian supporters as their team ran onto the pitch. Then the entire arena erupted as Billy Wales, the famous ram mascot of the Welsh Guards, was led out from the players' tunnel. The big Welsh captain came next, holding a tiny red-shirted boy by the hand as he led his team to line up for the royal presentation.

The smiling prince went along the line, shaking the hands of players on both teams, saying a word here and there. Once he was escorted back to his seat the band of the Welsh Guards struck up the first bars of the Italian national anthem and the Italian fans in the arena roared out the words to encourage their team. There were cheers as it ended, but a hush fell as the band played the first chords of the Welsh national anthem and every Welsh man, woman and child in the stadium, including those in the home team line-up not too choked with emotion, sang in one voice. Hairs rose on every patriotic neck present as the sound filled the stadium.

But through it all, even as she hugged Meg in triumph, one part of Alicia's brain was still numb with shock from confrontation with Francesco da Luca. She had known only too well that he might come here to support his country in such an important match. But in the throes of the Six Nations season there was no way she could have taken time off from her job today purely on the off-chance that he might turn up. Even less explain why. None of her colleagues knew about her connection to Francesco.

WIN A LUXURY
WEEKEND IN LONDON!

**We've got a luxury weekend stay at the
Home of England Rugby up for grabs
in every edition of the International
Billionaires mini-series(x 8).**

You and a partner will be treated to two nights'
accommodation in the brand-new London
Marriott Hotel Twickenham, where you'll
receive a free tour of the famous stadium, as
well as entry to the World Rugby Museum.

You'll also each come away with a free goody bag,
packed with books, England Rugby clothing
and other accessories.

INTERNATIONAL BILLIONAIRES

To enter, complete the entry form below and send to:
Mills & Boon RFU/May Prize Draw,
Eton House, 18-24 Paradise Road,
Richmond, Surrey, TW9 1SR

Mills & Boon® Rugby Prize Draw (May)

Name: _____

Address: _____

Post Code: _____

Daytime Telephone No: _____

E-mail Address: _____

❑ I have read the terms and conditions (please tick this box before entering).

❑ Please tick here if you do not wish to receive special offers from
   Harlequin Mills & Boon Ltd.

Closing date for entries is 21st June 2009

Terms & Conditions

1. Draw open to UK and Eire residents aged 18 and over. No purchase necessary. One entry per household per prize draw only. 2. Prizes are non-transferable and no cash alternatives will be offered. 3. All travel expenses to and from Twickenham must be covered by the prize winner. 4. All prizes are subject to availability. Should any prize be unavailable, a prize of similar value will be substituted. 5. Employees and immediate family members of Harlequin Mills & Boon Ltd are not eligible to enter. 6. Prize winners will be randomly selected from the eligible entries received. No correspondence will be entered into and no entry returned. 7. To be eligible, all entries must be received by 21st June 2009. 8. Prize-winner notification will be made by e-mail or letter no later than 15 days after the deadline for entry. 9. No responsibility can be accepted for entries that are lost, delayed or damaged. Proof of postage cannot be accepted as proof of delivery. 10. If any winner notification or prize is returned as undeliverable, an alternative winner will be drawn from eligible entries. 11. Names of competition winners are available on request.

FREE

2 BOOKS AND A SURPRISE GIFT!

We would like to take this opportunity to thank you for reading this Mills & Boon® book by offering you the chance to take TWO more specially selected titles from the Modern™ series absolutely FREE! We're also making this offer to introduce you to the benefits of the Mills & Boon® Book Club™—

★ **FREE home delivery**
★ **FREE gifts and competitions**
★ **FREE monthly Newsletter**
★ **Books available before they're in the shops**
★ **Exclusive Mills & Boon Book Club offers**

Accepting these FREE books and gift places you under no obligation to buy; you may cancel at any time, even after receiving your free shipment. Simply complete your details below and return the entire page to the address below. You don't even need a stamp!

YES! Please send me 2 free Modern books and a surprise gift. I understand that unless you hear from me, I will receive 4 superb new titles every month for just £3.19 each, postage and packing free. I am under no obligation to purchase any books and may cancel my subscription at any time. The free books and gift will be mine to keep in any case.

P9ZEE

Ms/Mrs/Miss/Mr...Initials ....
                                                                        BLOCK CAPITALS PLEASE

Surname ....

Address ....

....

....Postcode ....

Send this whole page to:
The Mills & Boon Book Club, FREEPOST CN81, Croydon, CR9 3WZ